S0-AXR-140

FRANK HERBERT

DIRECT DESCENT

BERKLEY BOOKS, NEW YORK

DIRECT DESCENT

A Berkley Book/published by arrangement with
the author

PRINTING HISTORY
Ace trade edition / October 1980
Ace mass market edition / October 1981
Berkley edition / October 1985

ISBN: 0-425-08186-9

A BERKLEY BOOK ® TM 757,375

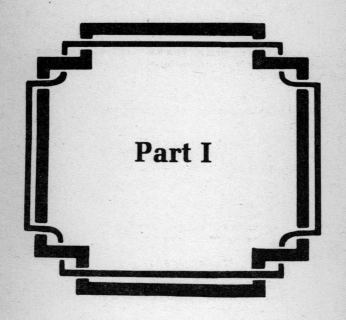

Part I

Vincent Coogan pulled at his thin lower lip as he stared at the image of his home planet growing larger in the star ship's viewscreen.

"What kind of an emergency would make Patterson call me off a Library collection trip?" he muttered.

The chief navigator turned toward Coogan, noted the down-drooping angles on the Library official's face. "Did you say something, sir?"

"Huh?" Coogan realized he had been speaking his thoughts aloud. He drew in a deep breath, squared his stringy frame in front of the viewscreen, said, "It's good to get back to the Library."

"Always good to be home," said the navigator. He turned toward the planet in the screen.

It was a garden world of rolling plains turning beneath an old sun. Pleasure craft glided across shallow seas. Villages of flat, chalk-white houses clustered around elevator towers which plumbed the interior. Slow streams meandered across the plains. Giant butterflies fluttered among trees and flowers. People walked while reading books or reclined with scan-all viewers hung in front of their eyes.

The star ship throbbed as its landing auxiliaries were activated. Coogan felt the power through his feet. Suddenly, he sensed the homecoming feeling in his chest, an anticipating that brought senses to new alertness. It was

enough to erase the worry over his call-back, to banish his displeasure at the year of work he had abandoned uncompleted.

It was enough to take the bitterness out of his thoughts when he recalled the words someone on an outworld had etched beside the star ship's main port. The words had been cut deeply beneath the winged boot emblem of the Galactic Library, probably with a Gernser flame chisel.

"Go home dirty pack rats!"

The *dirty pack rats* were home.

Director Caldwell Patterson of the Galactic Library sat at the desk in his office deep in the planet, a sheet of metallic paper in his hands. He was an old man even by Eighty-first Century standards when geriatrics made six hundred years a commonplace. Some said he had been *at* the Library that long. Gray hair clung in molting wisps to a pale pate. His face had the leathery, hook-nosed appearance of an ancient bird.

As Coogan entered the office, a desk visor in front of Patterson chimed. The director clicked a switch, motioned Coogan to a chair and said, "Yes," with a tired, resigned air.

Coogan folded his tall frame into the chair and listened with half his mind to the conversation on the visor. It seemed some outworld ship was approaching and wanted special landing

facilities. Coogan looked around the familiar office. Behind the director was a wall of panels, dials, switches, rheostats, speakers, microphones, oscillographs, code keys, screens. The two side walls were focus rhomboids for realized images. The wall which was split by the door held eight miniature viewscreens all tuned to separate channels of the Library information broadcasts. All sound switches had been turned to mute, leaving a continuous low murmur in the room.

Patterson began drumming his fingers on the desk top, glaring at the desk visor. Presently, he said, "Well, tell them we have no facilities for an honor reception. This planet is devoted to knowledge and research. Tell them to come in at the regular field. I'll obey my Code and any government order of which I'm capable, but we simply don't have the facilities for what they're asking." The director cut the switch on his visor, turned to Coogan. "Well, Vincent, I see you avoided the Hesperides green rot. Now I presume you're anxious to learn why I called you back from there?"

Same old didactic, pompous humbug, thought Coogan. He said, "I'm not exactly a robot," and shaped his mouth in a brief, wry smile.

A frown formed on Patterson's bluish lips. "We've a new government," he said.

"Is that why you called me in?" asked Coogan.

He felt an upsurge of all the resentment he'd swallowed when he'd received the call-back message.

"In a way, yes," said Patterson. "The new government is going to censor all Library broadcasts. The censor is on that ship just landing."

"They can't do that!" blurted Coogan. "The Charter expressly forbids chosen broadcasts or any interference with Library function! I can quote you—"

Patterson interrupted him in a low voice. "What is the first rule of the Library Code?"

Coogan faltered, stared at the director. He said, "Well—" paused while the memory came back to him. "The first rule of the Galactic Library Code is to obey all direct orders of the government in power. For the preservation of the Library, this must be the primary command."

"What does it mean?" demanded Patterson.

"It's just words that—"

"More than words!" said Patterson. A faint color crept into his old cheeks. "That rule has kept this Library alive for eight thousand years."

"But the government can't—"

"When you're as old as I am," said Patterson, "you'll realize that governments don't know what they can't do until after they cease to be governments. Each government carries the seeds of its own destruction."

"So we let them censor us," said Coogan.

"Perhaps," said Patterson, "if we're lucky. The new Grand Regent is the leader of the Gentle Ignorance Party. He says he'll censor us. The trouble is, our information indicates he's bent on destroying the Library as some kind of an example."

It took a moment for Coogan to accept the meaning of the words. "Destroy—"

"Put it to the torch," said Patterson. "His censor is his chief general and hatchetman."

"Doesn't he realize this is more than a Library?" asked Coogan.

"I don't know what he realizes," said Patterson. "But we're faced with a primary emergency and, to complicate matters, the entire staff is in a turmoil. They're hiding arms and calling in collection ships against my express orders. That Toris Sil-Chan has been around telling every—"

"Toris!"

"Yes, Toris. Your boon companion or whatever he is. He's leading this insurrection and I gather that he—"

"Doesn't he realize the Library can't fight a war without risking destruction?" asked Coogan.

Patterson sighed. "You're one of the few among the new generation who realizes that," he said.

"Where's Toris?" demanded Coogan. "I'll—"

"There isn't time right now," said Patterson. "The Grand Regent's hatchetman is due any minute."

"There wasn't a word of this out on Hesperides," said Coogan. "What's this Grand Regent's name?"

"Leader Adams," said Patterson.

"Never heard of him," said Coogan. "Who's the hatchetman?"

"His name's Pchak."

"Pchak what?"

"Just Pchak."

He was a coarse man with overdrawn features, none of the refinements of the inner worlds. A brown toga almost the same color as his skin was belted around him. Two slitted eyes stared out of a round, pushed-in face. He came into Patterson's office followed by two men in gray togas, each wearing a blaster at the belt.

"I am Pchak," he said.

Not a pretty specimen, thought Coogan. There was something chilling about the stylized simplicity of the man's dress. It reminded Coogan of a battle cruiser stripped down for action.

Director Patterson came around his desk, shoulders bent, walking slowly as befitted his age. "We are honored," he said.

"Are you?" asked Pchak. "Who is in command here?"

Patterson bowed. "I am Director Caldwell Patterson."

Pchak's lips twisted into something faintly like a smile. "I would like to know who is responsible for those insulting replies to our communications officer. *'This planet is devoted to knowledge and research!'* Who said that?"

"Why—" Patterson broke off, wet his lips with his tongue, "I said that."

The man in the brown toga stared at Patterson, said, "Who is this other person?" He hooked a thumb toward Coogan.

"This is Vincent Coogan," said Patterson. "He has just returned from the Hesperides Group to be on hand to greet you. Mr. Coogan is my chief assistant and successor."

Pchak looked at Coogan. "Out scavenging with the rest of the pack rats," he said. He turned back to Patterson. "But perhaps there will be need of a successor."

One of the guards moved up to stand beside the general. Pchak said, "Since knowledge is unhappiness, even the word is distasteful when used in a laudatory manner."

Coogan suddenly sensed something electric and deadly in the room. It was evident that Patterson did, too, because he looked directly at

Coogan and said, "We are here to obey."

"You demonstrate an unhappy willingness to admire knowledge," said Pchak.

The guard's blaster suddenly came up and chopped down against the director's head. Patterson slumped to the floor, blood welling from a gash on his scalp.

Coogan started to take a step forward, was stopped by the other guard's blaster prodding his middle. A red haze formed in front of Coogan's eyes, a feeling of vertigo swept over him. In spite of the dizziness, part of his mind went on clicking, producing information to be observed. *This is standard procedure for oppressors,* said his mind. *Cow your victims by an immediate show of violence.* Something cold, hard and calculating took over Coogan's consciousness.

"Director Coogan," said Pchak, "do you have any objections to what has just occurred?"

Coogan stared down at the squat brown figure. *I have to stay in control of the situation,* he thought. *I'm the only one left who'll fight this according to the Code.* He said, "Every man seeks advancement."

Pchak smiled. "A realist. Now explain your Library." He strode around the desk, sat down. "It hardly seems just for our government to maintain a pesthole such as this, but my orders are to investigate before passing judgment."

Your orders are to make a show of investigation before putting the Library to the torch, thought Coogan. He picked up an image control box from the desk, clipped it to his belt. Immediately, a blaster in a guard's hand prodded his side.

"What is that?" demanded Pchak.

Coogan swallowed. "These are image controls," he said. He looked down at Patterson sprawled on the floor. "May I summon a hospital robot for Mr. Patterson?"

"No," said Pchak. "What are image controls?"

Coogan took two deep breaths, looked at the side wall. "The walls of this room are focus rhomboids for realized images," he said. "They were turned off to avoid distractions during your arrival."

Pchak settled back in the chair. "You may proceed."

The guard continued to hold his blaster on Coogan.

Moving to a position opposite the wall, Coogan worked the belt controls. The wall became a window looking down an avenue of filing cases. Robots could be seen working in the middle distance.

"Terra is mostly a shell," said Coogan. "The major portion of the matter was taken to construct spaceships during the great outpouring."

"That fable again," said Pchak.

Coogan stopped. Involuntarily, his eyes went to the still figure of Caldwell Patterson on the floor.

"Continue," said Pchak.

The cold, hard, calculating something in Coogan's mind said, *You know what to do. Set him up for your Sunday punch.*

Coogan concentrating on the screen, said: "The mass loss was compensated by a giant gravitronic unit in the planet center. Almost the entire subsurface of Terra is occupied by the Library. Levels are divided into overlapping squares one hundred kilometers to the side. The wealth of records stored here staggers the imagination. It's—"

"Your imagination perhaps," said Pchak. "Not mine."

Coogan fought down a shiver which crawled along his spine, forced himself to continue. He said. "It is the repository for all the reported doings of every government in the history of the galaxy. The foremat was set by the original institution from which this one grew. It was known as the Library of Congress. That institution had a reputation of—"

"Congress," said Pchak in his deadly flat tones. "Kindly explain that term."

Now what have I said? Coogan wondered. He faced Pchak, said, "Congress was an ancient form of government. The closest modern example is the Tschi Council which—"

"I thought so!" barked Pchak. "That debating society! Would you explain to me, Mr. Coogan, why a recent Library broadcast extolled the virtures of this form of government?"

There's the viper, thought Coogan. He said, "Well, nobody watches Library broadcasts anyway. What with some five thousand channels pouring out—"

"Answer my question, Mr. Coogan." Pchak leaned forward. An eager look came into the eyes of the guard with the blaster. Again Coogan's eyes sought out the still form of Patterson on the floor.

"We have no control of program selection," said Coogan, "except on ten special channels for answering research questions and ten other channels which scan through the new material as it is introduced into the Library."

"No control," said Pchak. "That's an interesting answer. Why is this?"

Coogan rubbed the back of his neck with his left hand, said, "The charter for the broadcasts was granted by the first systemwide government in the Twenty-first Century. A method of random program selection was devised to insure impartiality. It was considered that the information in the Library should always be freely available to all—" His voice trailed off and he wondered if he had quoted too much of the charter. *Well, they can read it in the original if they want,* he thought.

"Fascinating," said Pchak. He looked at the nearest guard. "Isn't that so?"

The guard grinned.

Coogan took a slow, controlled breath, exhaled. He could feel a crisis approaching. It was like a weight on his chest.

"This has to be a thorough investigation," said Pchak. "Let's see what you're broadcasting right now."

Coogan worked the belt controls and an image realized before the righthand rhomboid. It was of a man with a hooked nose. He wore leather pants and shirt, shoes with some kind of animal face projecting from the toes, a feather crest hat on his head.

"This is a regular random information broadcast," said Coogan. He looked at his belt. "Channel Eighty-two." He turned up the volume.

The man was talking a language of harsh consonants punctuated by sibilant hisses. Beside him on the floor was a mound of tiny round objects, each bearing a tag.

"He is speaking the dead Procyon language," said Coogan. "He's a zoologist of a system which was destroyed by corona gas thirty-four centuries ago. The things on the floor are the skulls of a native rodent. he's saying that he spent eleven years classifying more than eight thousand of those skulls."

"Why?" asked Pchak. He seemed actually interested, leaned forward to look at the mound of skulls on the floor.

"I think we've missed that part," said Coogan. "It probably was to prove some zoological theory."

Pchak settled back in his chair. "He's dead," he said. "His system no longer exists. His language is no longer spoken. Is there much of this sort of thing being broadcast?"

"I'm afraid ninety-nine per cent of the Library broadcasts—excluding research channels—is of this nature," said Coogan. "It's the nature of the random selection."

"Who cares what the zoologist's theory was?" asked Pchak.

"Perhaps some zoologist," said Coogan. "You never can tell when a piece of information will be valuable."

Pchak muttered something under his breath which sounded like, "Pack rats!"

Coogan said, "Pack rats?"

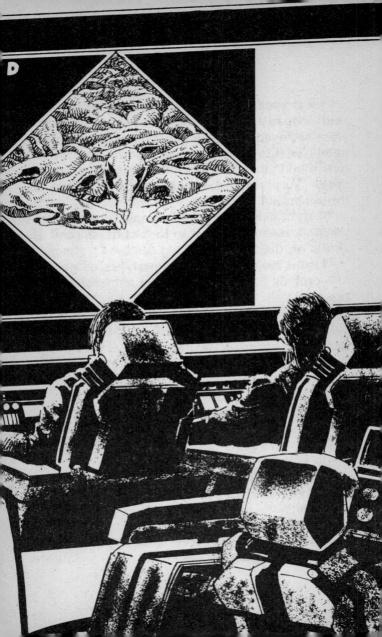

The little brown man smiled. "That's what we call you," he said. "And with some justification evidently. You're packed with the kind of useless material a rodent would admire."

Time for one small lesson, thought Coogan. He said, "The pack rat, also known as the trade rat, was a rodent indigenous to this planet. It's now extinct here, but there are examples on Markeb IX and several of the Ring planets. The pack rat lived in forest land and was known for his habit of stealing small things from hunters' camps. For everything it took, the pack rat left an item from its nest, a bit of twine, a twig, a shiny piece of glass, a rock. In all of that useless material which cluttered its nest there might be one nugget of a precious metal. Since the pack rat showed no selection in its trading—was random, so to speak—it might leave the precious metal in a hunter's camp in exchange for a bottle top."

Pchak got to his feet, walked across the room to the zoologist's image, passed a hand through the projection. "Remarkable," he said, sarcasm filling his voice. "This is supposed to be a nugget?"

"More likely a twig," said Coogan.

Pchak turned back, faced Coogan.

What else do you hide in this rat's nest? Any nuggets?"

Coogan looked down at Patterson on the floor. There was a stillness about the thin old figure.

"First, may I have a hospital robot attend to Mr. Patterson?"

The general kept his eyes on Coogan. "No. Answer my request."

First rule of the Code—obey, thought Coogan. With a slow, controlled movement, he shifted a lever on the box at his belt. The Procyon zoologist vanished and the wall became a screen showing a page of a book. *Here's the bait,* thought Coogan, *and I hope it poisons you.* He said, "This is an early account of military tactics showing some methods that succeeded and others that failed."

Pchak turned to the screen, put his hands behind him, rocked back and forth on heels and toes. "What language?"

"Ancient English of Terra," said Coogan. "We have a scanner that'll give you an oral translation if you'd like."

The general kept his eyes on the screen. "How do I know this account is accurate?"

"The Library Code does not permit tampering with records," said Coogan. "Our oath is to preserve the present for the future." He glanced at Pchak, back to the screen. "We have other battle records, the tactics of every species encountered by humans. For example, we have the entire war history of the Praemir of Roman II."

Coogan shifted his belt controls and the screen

took up a history of warfare which had been
assembled for a general sixteen centuries dead.
Pchak watched as the record went from clubs and
rocks to spears and made a side journey into
bizarre weapons. Suddenly, Coogan blanked the
screen.

Pchak's head snapped up. "Why did you stop
that?"

Hooked him, thought Coogan. He said, "I
thought you might rather view this at your lei-
sure. If you wish, I'll set up a viewing room and
show you how to order the records when there
are side issues you'd like to study." Coogan held
his breath. *Now we learn if he's really caught*, he
thought.

The general continued to study the blank screen. "I have orders to make a thorough investigation," he said. "I believe this comes under the
category of investigation. Have your viewing
room prepared." He turned, went to the door,
followed by his guards.

"It's down on the sixty-ninth level," said Coogan. "Viewing room A." He started toward
Pchak. "I'll get you all set up and—"

"You will remain here," said Pchak. "We will
use Viewing Room B, instead. Send an assistant
to explain things." He glanced back. "You do
have an assistant, do you not?"

"I'll send Toris Sil-Chan," said Coogan and

AX-270-B

then remembered what Patterson had said about Toris leading the hotheads who wanted to do battle. He would have bitten off his tongue to retract the words, but knew he dared not change now or it would arouse Pchak's suspicions. He returned to the desk, had central-routing find Toris and send him to the viewing room. *Please don't do anything rash,* he prayed.

"Is this assistant your successor?" asked Pchak, looking down at Patterson.

"No," said Coogan.

"You must appoint a successor," said Pchak and left with his two guards.

Coogan immediately summoned a hospital robot for Patterson. The scarab shape came in on silent wheels, lifted the still form on its flat pad extensors and departed.

The sunset rain was drifting along its longitudinal mark on Terra, spattering a shallow sea, dewing the grasslands, filling the cups of flowers. One wall screen of the director's office was activated to show this surface scene—a white village in the rain, flutterings of trees. Surface copters whirred across the village, their metal gleaming in the wetness.

Coogan, his thin face wearing a look of weariness, sat at the director's desk, hands clasped in front of him. Occasionally, he glanced at the wall screen. The spire of a government star ship—tall alabaster with a sunburst insignia on its bow—could be seen beyond the village. Coogan sighed.

A chime sounded behind him. He turned to the control panel wall, depressed a button, spoke into a microphone. "Yes?"

A voice like wire scraped across a tin plate came out of the speaker. "This is the hospital."

"Well?" Coogan's voice showed irritation.

"Director Patterson was dead upon arrival here," said the wire-scraping voice. "The robots already have disposed of his body through the CIB orifice."

"Don't say anything about it yet," said Coogan. He removed his hand from the switch, turned back to the desk. *His* desk now. *Director Coogan.* The thought gave him no satisfaction. He kept remembering a still form sprawled on the floor. *A terrible way to go,* he thought. *A Librarian should end at his researches, just quietly topple over in the stacks.*

The desk visor chimed. Coogan hit the palm switch and Pchak's face appeared on the screen. The general was breathing rapidly, beads of sweat on his forehead.

"May I help you?" asked Coogan.

"How do I get the condemned instruction records for the Zosma language?" demanded Pchak. "Your machine keeps referring me to some non-

sense about abstract symbolism."

The door of Coogan's office opened and Sil-Chan entered, saw that a caller was on the screen, stopped just inside the door. Sil-Chan was a blocky figure who achieved fat without looking soft. His round face was dominated by upswept almond eyes characteristic of the inhabitants of the Mundial Group planets of Ruchbah.

Coogan shook his head at Sil-Chan, his mind searching through memories for an answer to Pchak's question. It came to him, tagged *semantics study*. "Zosma," he said. "Yes, that was a language which dealt only in secondary referents. Each phrase was two times removed from—"

"What in Shandu is a secondary referent?" exploded Pchak.

Calmly, thought Coogan. *I can't afford to precipitate action yet.* He said, "Ask for the section on semantics. Did Mr. Sil-Chan show you how to get the records you need?"

"Yes, yes," said Pchak. "Semantics, eh?" The screen went blank.

Sil-Chan closed the door, came across the office. "I would imagine," he said, "that the general is under the impression his researches will be completed in a week or two."

"So it would seem," said Coogan. He studied

Sil-Chan. The man didn't look like a hothead, but perhaps it had taken this threat to the Library to set him off.

Sil-Chan took a chair across from Coogan. "The general is a low alley dog," he said, "but he believes in this Leader Adams. The gleam in his eyes when he talks about Adams would frighten a saint."

"How was it down in the viewing room?" asked Coogan.

"Pchak is busy studying destruction," said Sil-Chan. "We haven't made up our minds yet whether to exterminate him. Where's Director Patterson?"

A sixth sense warned Coogan not to reveal that the director was dead. He said, "He isn't here."

"That's fairly obvious," said Sil-Chan. "I have an ultimatum to deliver to the director. Where is he?"

"You can deliver your ultimatum to me," said Coogan dryly.

Sil-Chan's eyes showed little glints deep in the pupils as he stared at Coogan. "Vince, we've been friends a long time," he said, "but you've been away in the Hesperides Group and don't know what's been going on here. Don't take sides yet."

"What's been going on?" asked Coogan. He looked up at Sil-Chan out of the corners of his eyes.

The Mundial native hitched himself forward and leaned an elbow on the desk. "There's a new government, Vince, and they're planning to destroy the Library. And that gourd-head Patterson has been giving in to every order they send. Do this! Do that! He does it! He told us flat out he wouldn't defy a government order." Sil-Chan's mouth set in a thin line. "*It's against the Library Code!*"

"Who is *we*?" asked Coogan.

"Huh?" Sil-Chan looked blank.

"The *we* you said hasn't decided whether to exterminate Pchak," said Coogan.

"Oh." Sil-Chan leaned back. "Only about a third of the home staff. Most of the collection crews are joining us fast as they come in."

Coogan tapped a finger against the desk. *Some eight thousand people, more or less,* he thought. He said, "What's your plan?"

"Easy." Sil-Chan shrugged. "I've about fifty men in Section 'C' on the sixty-ninth level waiting for the word to move against Pchak and his bodyguards. Another three hundred are topside ready to jump the government ship."

Coogan tipped his head to one side and stared at Sil-Chan in amazement. "Is that your ultimatum?"

Sil-Chan shook his head. "No. Where's Patterson?"

Something decisive meshed in Coogan's mind. He got to his feet. "Patterson's dead. I'm director. What's your ultimatum?"

There was a moment's silence with Sil-Chan looking up at Coogan. "How'd he die?" asked Sil-Chan.

"He was old," said Coogan. "What's your ultimatum?"

Sil-Chan wet his lips with his tongue. "I'm sorry to hear that, Vince." Again he shrugged. "But this makes our job simpler. You're a man who'll listen to reason." He met Coogan's stare. "This is our plan. We take over this Pchak and his ship, hold him as hostage while we convert every broadcast channel we have to public support. With five thousand channels telling the—"

"You bone-brain!" barked Coogan.

"That's as stupid a plan as I've ever heard. Adams would ignore your hostage and drop a stellar bomb in our laps!"

"But, Vince—"

"Don't but, Vince, me," said Coogan. He came around the desk and stood over Sil-Chan. "As long as you're running around disobeying the orders of your superiors you'll refer to me as Mr. Director and—"

Sil-Chan charged to his feet, glared up at Coogan. "I hate to do this, Vince," he said, "but we have organization and purpose. You can't stop

us! You're relieved of your directorship until such time as—"

"Shut up!" Coogan strode around behind his desk, put his hand on a short lever low on the control panel. "Do you know what this is, Toris?"

Sil-Chan's face showed uncertainty. He shook his head.

"This is the master control for the gravitronic unit," said Coogan. "If I push it down, it shuts off the unit. Every bit of soil, everything beyond the Library shell will drift off into space."

A pasty color came over Sil-Chan's features. He put out a hand toward Coogan. "You can't do that," he said. "Your wife and family—all of our families are up there. They wouldn't have a chance!"

"I'm director here," said Coogan. "The position is my earned right!" With his free hand, he moved four switches on the control wall. "That seals off your sixty-ninth level group behind fire panels." He turned back to Sil-Chan. "Now, get in touch with every insurgent under you and have them turn in their arms to robots which I'll release for the job. I know who some of your men are. They'd better be among the ones you contact. If you make one move I don't like, this lever goes down and stays down!"

"You!" said Sil-Chan. He ground his teeth to-

gether. "I knew I should've carried a blaster when I came in here. But no! You and Patterson were the civilized types! We could reason with you!"

"Start making those calls," said Coogan. He pushed his desk visor toward the other man.

Sil-Chan jerked the visor to him, obeyed. Coogan gave his orders to robot dispatching headquarters, waited for Sil-Chan to finish. The Mundial native finally pushed the visor back across the desk. "Does that satisfy you?" he demanded.

"No." Coogan steepled his hands in front of him. "I'm arming some of the staff I can trust. Their orders will be to shoot to kill if there's a further act of insurrection." He leaned forward. "In addition, we're going to have guard stations between sectors and a regular search procedure. You're not getting another chance to cause trouble."

Sil-Chan clenched and unclenched his fists. "And what do you intend to do about this Pchak and his Leader Adams?"

"They're the government," said Coogan. "As such the Code requires that we obey their orders. I will obey their orders. And, any man on the staff who even hints at disobedience, I'll personally turn over to Pchak for disciplinary action."

Sil-Chan arose slowly. "I've known you more

than sixty years, Mr. Coogan. That just shows how little you can learn about a rat. After you've lost the Library to this madman, you won't have a friend left here. Not me, not the people who trust you now. Not your wife or your family." He sneered. "Why—one of your own sons, Phil, is in with us." He pointed a finger at Coogan. "I intend to tell everyone about the threat you used today to gain control of the Library."

"Control of the Library is my earned right," said Coogan. He smiled, pushed down the lever in the control wall. The wall made a quarter turn on a central pivot. "Toris, send up a repair robot when you report back to Pchak. I've special installations I want to make here."

Sil-Chan came to the edge of the desk, staring down at the lever which had controlled the movement of the wall. "Tricked me!"

"You tricked yourself," said Coogan. "You did it the moment you turned your back on our greatest strength—obedience to the government."

Sil-Chan grunted, whirled and left the office.

Coogan watched the door as it closed behind the other man, thought, *If I only had as much faith in those words as I'm supposed to have.*

She was a pretty woman with hair like glowing coals, small features except for a wide, sensual mouth. Her green eyes seemed to give off sparks to match her hair as she stared out of the visor at Coogan.

"Vince, where have you been?" she demanded.

He spoke in a tired voice. "I'm sorry, Fay. I had work that had to be done."

She said, "The boys brought their families from Antigua for a reunion and we've been ready for you for hours. What's going on? What's this nonsense Toris is bleating?"

Coogan sighed and brushed a hand through his hair. "I don't know what Toris is saying. But the Library is in a crisis. Patterson is dead and I've nobody I can trust to hold things together."

Her eyes went wide; she put a hand to her mouth, spoke through her fingers. "Oh, no! Not Pat!"

"Yes," he said.

"How?"

"I guess it was too much for him," said Coogan. "He was old."

"I couldn't believe Toris," she said.

Coogan felt a great weariness just at the edge of his mind. "You said the boys are there," he said. "Ask Phil if he was part of the group backing Toris."

"I can tell you myself he was," she said. "It's no secret. Darling, what's come over you? Toris said you threatened to dump the whole surface off

into space."

"It was an empty threat then," said Coogan. "Toris was going to disobey the government. I couldn't permit it. That would only—"

"Vince! Have you gone out of your mind?" Her eyes registered amazement and horror. "This Adams means to destroy the Library! We can't just sit back and let him!"

"We've grown lax in our training." said Coogan. "We've had it too easy for too long. That's a situation I intend to correct!"

"But what about—"

"If I'm permitted to handle things my way, he won't destroy the Library," said Coogan. "I was hoping you'd trust me."

"Of course I trust you, darling, but—"

"Then trust me," he said. "And please understand that there's no place I'd rather be right now than home with you."

She nodded. "Of course, dear."

"Oh, yes," he aid, "tell Phil he's under house arrest for deliberate disobedience to the Code. I'll deal with him, personally, later." He closed the switch before she could reply.

Now for General Pchak, he thought. *Let's see if he can give us a hint on how to deal with Leader Adams.*

The room was vaguely egg-shaped for acoustical reasons, cut at one end by the flat surface of a screen and with space in the center for a realized image. The wall opposite the screen was occupied by a curved couch split by drop arms in which control instruments were set.

Pchak was sprawled on the couch, a brown blob against the gray plastic, watching two Krigëllian gladiators spill each other's blood in an arena which had a shifting floor. As Coogan entered, Pchak turned the screen to a book page in the Zosma language of Krigëllia, scanned a few lines. He looked up at Coogan with an expression of irritation.

"Director Coogan," said Pchak, "have you chosen a successor yet?" He slid his feet to the floor. "I find semantics most interesting, Director Coogan. The art of using words as weapons appeals to me. I'm particularly interested in psychological warfare."

Coogan stared thoughtfully at the figure in the brown toga, an idea racing through his mind. If I get this barbarian started on a study of psychological warfare, he'll never leave. He pulled out a section of the curved couch, sat down facing Pchak. "What's the most important thing to know about a weapon?" he asked.

The general's forehead creased. "How to use it effectively, of course."

Coogan shook his head. "That's an overgeneral-

ization. The most important thing is to know your weapon's limitations."

Pchak's eyes widened. "What it *cannot* do. Very clever."

"Psychological warfare is an extensive subject," said Coogan. "According to some, it's a two-edged sword with no handle. If you grasp it strongly enough to strike down your enemy, you render yourself *hors de combat* before your blow is delivered."

Pchak leaned against an arm of the couch. "I don't believe I understand you."

Coogan said, "Well, the whole argument is specious, anyway. You'd first have to apply the methods of psychology to yourself. As you measured more and more of your own sanity, you'd be more and more incapable of using the weapon against another."

In a cold voice, Pchak said, "Are you suggesting that I'm insane?"

"Of course not," said Coogan. "I'm giving you a summary of one of the arguments about psychological warfare. Some people believe any warfare is insanity. But sanity is a matter of degree. Degree implies measurement. To measure, we must use some absolute referent. Unless we could agree on the measuring device, we couldn't say anyone was sane or insane. Nor could we tell what opponent might be vulnerable to our weapon."

Pchak jerked forward, a hard light in his slitted eyes.

Coogan hesitated, wondered, *Have I gone too far?* He said, "I'll give you another example." He hooked a thumb toward the viewscreen. "You just watched two gladiators settle an issue for their cities. That particular action occurred twenty centuries ago. You weren't interested in the issue they settled. You were examining their method of combat. Twenty centuries from now, who will examine your methods? Will they be interested in the issues you settled?"

Pchak turned his head to one side, keeping his eyes on Coogan. "I think you're using clever words in a way to confuse me," he said.

"No, general," Coogan shook his head. "We're not here to confuse people. We believe in our Code and live by it. That Code says we must obey the government. And that doesn't mean we obey when we feel like it or when we happen to agree with you. We obey. Your orders will be carried out. It doesn't pay us to lead you into confusion."

In a strangely flat voice, Pchak said, "Knowledge is a blind alley leading only to unhappiness."

Coogan suddenly realized that the man was quoting Leader Adams. He said, "We don't put out knowledge, general. We store information.

That's our first job."

"But you blat that information all over the universe!" stormed the general. "Then it becomes knowledge!"

"That is under the Charter, not the Code," said Coogan.

Pchak pursed his lips, leaned toward Coogan. "Do you mean if I ordered you to shut down your broadcasts, you'd just do it? We understood you were prepared to resist us at every turn."

"Then your information was incorrect," said Coogan.

The general leaned back, rubbed his chin. "All right, shut them down," he said. "I'll give you a half hour. I want all five thousand of them quiet and your special channels, too."

Coogan bowed, got to his feet. "We obey," he said.

In the director's office Coogan sat at the desk, staring at the opposite wall. The screens were silent. It was almost as though there was some interspatial hole in the room, a lack. The door opened and Sil-Chan entered. "You sent for me?" he asked.

Coogan looked at the man for a moment before speaking, then aid, "Why didn't you return to Pchak's viewing room as I ordered?"

"Because Pchak dismissed me," said Sil-Chan

curtly.

"Come in and sit down," said Coogan. He turned on his desk visor, called records. "What's the parentage and upbringing of the new Grand Regent?" he asked.

After a brief pause, a voice came from the visor: "Leader Adams, also known as Adam Yoo. Mother, Simila Yoo, native of Mundial Group"—Coogan glanced at Sil-Chan—"planet Sextus C III. Father Princeps Adams, native of Hercules Group. Father was killed in accident with subspace translator on University Planet of Hercules XII when son age nine. Young Adams raised with mother's family on Sextus C II until age eighteen when sent to Shandu for training as a Mundial religious leader. While on Shandu—"

Coogan interrupted, "Send me a transcript on it." He broke the connection, looked at Sil-Chan. "Still angry, Toris?"

Sil-Chan's lips tightened.

As though he had not noticed, Coogan said, "Adams' father was killed in an accident on a university planet. That could be the unconscious origin of his hatred of knowledge." He looked speculatively at Sil-Chan. "You're a Mundial native. What's the group like?"

"If Adams was raised there, he's a mystic," said Sil-Chan. He shrugged. "All of our people are mystics. No Mundial family would permit otherwise. That's why he was taken to the home planet to be raised." Sil-Chan suddenly put a hand to his chin. "Father killed in an accident—" He looked at Coogan, through him. "That could have been an *arranged* accident." He leaned forward, tapped the desk. "Let's say the father objected to the son being raised in the Mundial Group—"

"Are you suggesting that the mother could have arranged the accident?"

"Either she or some of her kinsmen," said Sil-Chan. "It's been known to happen. The Mundials are jealous of their own. I had the glax of a time getting permission to come to the Library staff."

"This happiness through ignorance cult," said Coogan. "How would mysticism bear on that?"

Sil-Chan looked at the desk surface, forehead creased. "He'll believe absolutely in his own destiny. If he thinks he has to destroy the Library to fulfill that destiny, there'll be no stopping him."

Coogan clasped his hands together on the desk top, gripped them until they hurt. *Obey!* he thought. *What a weapon to use against a fanatic!*

"If we could prove the mother or the Yoo Clan had the father killed, that might be a valuable piece of knowledge," said Sil-Chan.

"A wise man depends upon his friends for information and upon himself for decisions," said Coogan.

"That's a Mundial axiom," said Sil-Chan.

"I read it somewhere," said Coogan. "You're a Mundial native, Toris. Explain this mysticism."

"It's mostly rubbed off of me," said Sil-Chan, "but I'll try. It revolves around an ancient form of ancestor worship. Mysticism, you see, is the art of looking backward while convincing yourself that you're looking forward. The ancient Terran god Janus was a mystic. He looked forward and backward at the same time. Everything a mystic does in the present must find its interpretation in the past. Now, the interpretation—"

"That's a subtle one," said Coogan. "It almost slipped past me. *Interpretation.* Substitute *explanation* for *interpretation—*"

"And you have a librarian," said Sil-Chan.

"Explanation is something that may or may not be true," said Coogan. "We're convinced of an interpretation."

"Semantics again," said Sil-Chan. A brief smile touched his lips. "Maybe that's why you're director."

"Still against me?" asked Coogan.

The smile left Sil-Chan's mouth. "It's suicide, Vince." He hitched himself forward. "If we follow your orders, when this Adams says to destroy the Library, we'd have to help him!"

"So we would," said Coogan. "But it's not going to come to that. I wish you'd trust me, Toris."

"If you were doing something that even remotely made sense, of course I would," said Sil-Chan. "But-—" He shrugged.

"I've a job for you," said Coogan. "It may or may not make sense, but I want it carried out to the letter. Take any ship you can get and hop to this Sextus C III in the Mundial Group. When you get there, I want you to prove that the Yoo Clan killed Leader Adams' father. I don't care whether it's true or not. I want the proof."

"That makes sense," said Sil-Chan. "If we can discredit the big boss—"

The visor chimed. Coogan hit the switch and a sub-librarian's face appeared in the screen. "Sir," the man blurted, "the Library information broadcasts are silent! I just got a call from—"

"Orders of the government," said Coogan. "It's quite all right. Return to your duties." He blanked the screen.

Sil-Chan was leaning on the desk, fists clenched. "You mean you let them close us down without a struggle."

"Let me remind you of some things," said Coogan. "We must obey the government to survive. I am director here and I've given you an order. Get on it!"

"What if I refuse?"

"I'll get somebody else to do it and you'll be locked up."

"You don't leave me any choice." He turned and slammed out of the office.

Twenty-four times the evening rains passed across the tower far above Coogan's office. The game of cat-and-mouse with Pchak went on as usual, the little brown general delving deeper and deeper into the files. On the twenty-fifth day Coogan came into his office in mid afternoon.

Pchak is completely hooked, he thought, *but what happens when Adams finds out the Library hasn't been destroyed?*

He sat down at his desk, swiveled to face the control panel and activated a tiny screen linked to a spy cell on the sixty-ninth level. Pchak was in the viewing room, studying the Albireo language preexamining that double-star system's war history. Behind Coogan, a mechanical hum sounded, indicating someone was emerging from the elevator. Hastily, he blanked the spy screen, turned to his desk just as the door burst open. Toris Sil-Chan staggered into the room, his clothing torn, a dirty bandage over one shoulder.

The Mundial native lurched across the room, clutched the edge of Coogan's desk. "Hide me!" he said. "Quick!"

Coogan jerked around to the panel, swung it open and motioned toward the hole that was exposed. Sil-Chan darted in and Coogan closed the panel, returned to his desk.

Again the telltale signaled. Two armed guards burst into the room, blasters in their hands. "Where is he?" demanded the first.

"Where's who?" asked Coogan. He squared a stack of papers on his desk.

"The guy who jumped off that lifeboat," said the guard.

"I don't know what you're talking about," said Coogan, "but I can see that I'll have to call General Pchak and tell him how you've burst into my office without preamble and—"

The guard lowered his blaster and retreated one step. "That won't be necessary, sir," he said. "We can see the man's not here. He probably went to a lower level. Please excuse the interruption." They backed out of the room.

Coogan waited until his spy relays in the corridor told him the men had gone, then opened the panel. Sil-Chan was crumpled on the floor. Coogan bent over him, shook him. "Toris! What's wrong?"

Sil-Chan stirred, looked up at Coogan with eyes that were at first unrecognizing. "Uh . . . Vince—"

The director put an arm behind Sil-Chan, supported the man to a sitting position. "Take it easy now. Just tell me what happened."

"Made a mess of assignment," said Sil-Chan. "Yoo Clan got wind of what I was after. Had Adams send order . . . arrest. Lost ship. Got away in escape boat. Landed other side . . . planet. Pchak's guards tried stop—" His head slumped forward.

Coogan put a hand to the man's heart, felt its steady pumping. He eased Sil-Chan back to the floor, went out and summoned a hospital robot. Sil-Chan regained consciousness while the robot was listing him. "Sorry to go out on you like that," he said. "I—"

The message visor on the director's desk chimed. Coogan pushed the response switch, scanned the words of a visual message, blanked the screen and turned back to Sil-Chan. "You'll have to be treated here," he said. "Couldn't risk carrying you through the corridors right now.

The spy beam hummed at the door. Coogan pushed Sil-Chan behind the panel, closed it. Pchak strode into the office, a blaster in his hand, thw two guards behind him. The general glanced at the hospital robot, looked at Coogan. "Where's the man that robot was called to treat?"

The last guard into the office closed the door, drew his blaster.

"Talk or you'll be cut down where you stand," said Pchak. *The showdown*, thought Coogan. He said, "These hospital robots are a peculiar kind of creature, general. They don't have the full prime directive against harming humans because sometimes they have to choose between saving one person and letting another one die. I can tell this robot that if I'm harmed it must give all of you an overdose of the most virulent poison it carried in its hypo arm. I informed the robot that this action will save my life. It naturally is loyal to the Library and will do exactly what I have just now told it to do."

Pchak's face tightened. He raised the blaster slightly.

"Unless you wish to die in agony, place your blasters on my desk," said Coogan.

"I won't," said Pchak. "Now what're you going to do?"

"Your blasters can kill me," said Coogan, "but they won't stop that robot until it has carried out my order."

Pchak's finger began to tighten on the trigger. "Then let's give it the—"

The sharp *blat!* of an energy bolt filled the room. Pchak slumped. The guard behind him skirted the robot fearfully, put his blaster on Coogan's desk. The weapon smelled faintly of ozone from the blast that had killed Pchak. "Call

that thing off me now," said the man, staring at the robot.

Coogan looked at the other guard. "You, too," he said.

The other man came around behind the robot, put his weapon on the desk. Coogan picked up one of the weapons. It felt strange in his hand.

"You're not going to turn that thing loose on us now, are you?" asked the second guard. He seemed unable to take his gaze from the robot.

Coogan glanced down at the scarab shape of the mechanical with its flat pad extensors and back hooks for carrying a stretcher. He wondered what the two men would do if he told them the thing Pchak had undoubtedly known—that the robot could take no overt action against a human, that his words had been a lie.

The first guard said, "Look, we're on your side now. We'll tell you everything. Just before he came down here, Pchak got word that Leader Adams was coming and—"

"Adams!" Coogan barked the word. He thought, *Adams coming! How to turn that to advantage?* He looked at the first guard. "You were with Pchak when he came the first day, weren't you?"

"I was his personal guard," said the man.

Coogan scooped the other blaster off his desk, backed away. "All right. When Adams lands, ycu get on that visor and tell him Pchak wishes to see him down here. With Adams a hostage, I can get the rest to lay down their arms."

"But—" said the guard.

"One false move and I turn that robot loose on you," said Coogan.

The guard's throat worked visibly. He said, "We'll do it. Only I don't see how you can get the whole government to give up just because—"

"Then stop thinking," said Coogan. "Just get Adams down here." He backed against the control wall and waited.

"I don't understand," said Sil-Chan.

The Mundial native sat in a chair across the desk from Coogan. A fresh Library uniform bulged over Sil-Chan's bandaged shoulder. "You pound it into us that we have to obey," he said. "You tell us we can't go against the Code. Then at the last minute you turn around and throw a blaster on the whole crew and toss them into the hospital's violent ward."

"I don't think they can get out of there," said Coogan.

"Not with all those guards around them," said Sil-Chan. "But it's still disobedience and that's against the Code." He held up a hand, palm toward Coogan. "Not that I'm objecting, you understand. It's what I was advocating all along."

"That's where you're mistaken," said Coogan. "People were perfectly willing to ignore the Library and its silly broadcasts as long as that information was available. Then the broadcasts were stopped by government order."

"But—" Sil-Chan shook his head.

"There's another new government," said Coogan. "Leader Adams was booted out because he told people they couldn't have something. That's bad policy for a politician. They stay in office by telling people they can *have* things."

Sil-Chan said, "Well, where does—"

"Right, after you came stumbling in here," said Coogan, "I received a general order from the new government which I was only too happy to obey. It said that Leader Adams was a fugitive and any person encountering him was empowered to arrest him and hold him for trial." Coogan arose, strode around to Sil-Chan, who also got to his feet. "So you see," said Coogan, "I did it all by obeying the government."

The Mundial native glanced across Coogan's desk, suddenly smiled and went around to the control wall. "And you got me with a tricky thing like this lever." He put a hand on the lever with which Coogan had forced his submission.

Coogan's foot caught Sil-Chan's hand and kicked it away before the little man could depress the lever.

Sil-Chan backed away, shaking his bruised hand. "Ouch!" He looked up at Coogan. "What in the name of—"

The director worked a lever higher on the wall and the panel made a quarter turn. He darted behind the wall, began ripping wires from a series of lower connections. Presently, he stepped out. There were beads of perspiration on his forehead.

Sil-Chan stared at the lever he had touched. "Oh, no—" he said. "You didn't *really* hook that to the grav unit!"

Coogan nodded mutely.

Eyes widening, Sil-Chan backed against the desk, sat on it. "Then you weren't certain obedience would work, that—"

"No, I wasn't," growled Coogan.

Sil-Chan smiled. "Well, now, there's a piece of information that ought to be worth something." The smile widened to a grin. "What's my silence worth?"

The director slowly straightened his shoulders. He wet his lips with his tongue. "I'll tell you, Toris. Since you were to get this position anyway, I'll tell you what it's worth to me." Coogan smiled, a slow, knowing smile that made Sil-Chan squint his eyes.

"You're my successor," said Coogan.

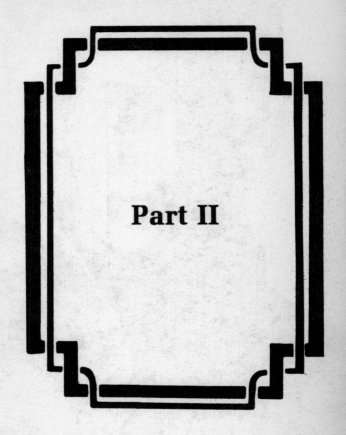

Part II

Whenever Sooma Sil-Chan moved along these lower corridors of the Library Planet, he liked to think of his ancestors marching through these ancient spaces. Family history was a special favorite in his studies and he felt that he knew all of those people intimately, their crises, their victories—all preserved in the archival records these thousands of years. His thirty-times removed grandfather, Toris, had paced along this very corridor every day of that long-gone life.

Robot menials made way for him and Sooma knew that at least *parts* of some of these very robots had made way for that other Sil-Chan. The menials were manufactured to last. There was one of them down in his own office, Archival Chief Accountancy, that was known to have gone without need of repair for twenty-one human generations.

The fandoor of the Director's office opened before him and Sooma Sil-Chan put on his best mask of efficiency. There had been no hint at why Director Patterson Tchung had summoned the Chief Accountant. It was probably some simple matter, but Tchung was notorious as a boring stickler for detail. The Director's mouth apparently could ramble on for hours while all around him battled ennui.

Sil-Chan stepped into the Director's presence, heard the fandoor seal.

Patterson Tchung sat behind his glistening desk like an ancient simian, his characteristic scowl reduced to a squinting of the brown eyes. Wisps of black hair trailed across Tchung's mostly-bald pate and his thin lips were drawn into a tight line which Sil-Chan could not interpret. Disapproval?

Even before Sil-Chan took a seat across from him, Tchung began speaking:

"Terrible problem, Sooma. Terrible."

Sil-Chan eased himself into the cushioned chair carefully. He had never heard that tone from Tchung before. Sil-Chan cast a quick look around the Director's office, wondering if it contained evidence of this "Terrible problem." The walls which were focus rhomboids for realized images had been silenced. They presented a uniform silver grey. The only touches of color in the office were behind the Director—a low table cluttered with curios, each one a story from some far-ranging collection ship of this "Pack Rat Planet." There was a gold statuette from the Researchers of Naos, an arrow thorn from Jacun, a tiny mound of red Atikan whisper seeds in their ceremonial fiber cup of gleaming purple . . . even an Eridanus fire scroll with its flameletters . . .

"Terrible," Tchung repeated. "We will be destroyed within six months unless we solve it.

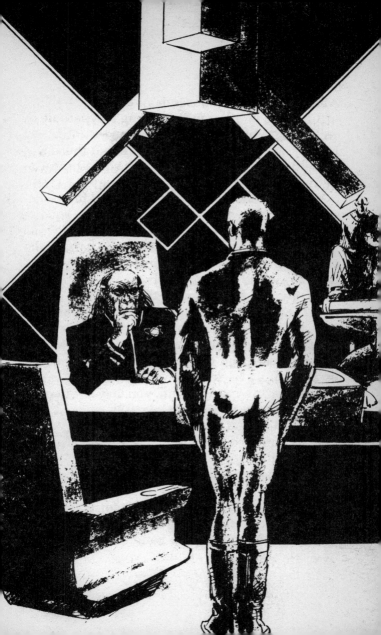

After all of these thousands of years . . . this!"

Sil-Chan, familiar with Tchung's hyperbole as well as with his ability to bore even the dullest of Library workers, wanted to smile, but there was something in Tchung's manner, something undefinably odd.

Tchung leaned forward and studied his assistant. Sil-Chan was a large man with a square, rather handsome face, green eyes under brows so blonde as to be almost invisible. His hair, of the same pale ivory, was close cropped, a new fashion among the youner archivists.

Misgivings began to fill the Director's mind. *Can this be the man upon whom our survival depends?* The nostrils of Tchung's high-ridged nose flared briefly, his eyes opened wide. He took a deep breath and calmed himself. There could be no turning back.

"Sooma, my young friend, you may be our only hope," Tchung said.

"What? I don't . . ."

"Of course you don't. But those government accountants who . . ."

"Those jackals I've been guiding through our files?"

"Those accountants," Tchung corrected him.

"Have I done something wrong? I mean . . ."

"No!" Tchung passed a hand over his eyes. "I must obey and yet I cannot."

Now, Sil-Chan saw at least the core of Tchung's disturbance. Galactive Archives—this Library Planet —had existed for thousands of years by the absolute dictum that its workers must obey the government—no matter the government. The accountants from the current government had descended upon them a fortnight ago, sneering at the "Pack Rats," demanding this record and that record. Something about that event had created a dilemma for Tchung.

"What's the problem?" Sil-Chan asked.

"Those accountants came from a war monitor which is parked in orbit above us. Accountants do not need a war monitor."

Sil-Chan stared at the Director in silence. *Was that it?* Could that possibly constitute the essence of Tchung's upset? Sil-Chan thought of a giant war monitor circling over the park-like surface of this unique planet. Up there lay serenity and open vistas, forests and lakes and rivers—even a few low mountains. But down here, in fact all the way to the planet's core, was a honeycombed hive of storage and recording activity. The Library collection ships went out and came back with their information and their curios. The random-selection system at the heart of the planet's activity, chosen from all of that accumulated material and broadcast thousands of programs daily all across the known universe—a bit of this and a bit of that, sometimes interesting, but mostly boring . . . just as boring as old Tchung here.

"That does not strike me as necessarily a terrible problem," Sil-Chan said.

"There is more. Believe me, there is more."

Tchung wondered how he could unfold the problem for the younger man and still keep Sil-Chan obedient to the code. It was such a complex problem . . .

Sil-Chan sighed. Better men than he had despaired of ever bringing Tchung directly to the point. The man was a committed wanderer. And if the presence of a war monitor was all that. . . .

For his part, Tchung's thoughts were on the government accountants in their cell-like rooms of this hive planet—the eager men pouring over Archival records, bent on paring down the budget until this ancient institution died. And those men were on the trail of the things they needed.

"I am forced to remind you of our Code," Tchung said. "Obedience to government. That one rule has kept us alive through crisis after crisis and through more than five thousand governments."

"The Code, yes. I saw that you . . ."

"We are here to preserve the present for the future—any present for any future. Wherever the curiosity of our collectors takes them, that is what we preserve."

"All right! What has happened?"

"Although this crisis may very well be our last one, Sooma, you are to do nothing, think nothing, say nothing that may be construed even remotely as disobedience to the government."

"Agreed! Agreed!"

"Patience, my young friend. Patience."

Again, Tchung covered his eyes with a hand. *This is the tool upon which I depend. This childless . . . bachelor . . . so intent upon his career that he has no time for home and mate . . . no thoughts at all for the long endurance which is the survival of us all. This youth . . . this callow . . . He's not yet fifty and he . . .*

"Are you ill, sir?" Sil-Chan asked.

Tchung lowered his hand, opened his eyes. "No. You were correct, of course, to call those accountants jackals. They will feast themselves on anything. They mean to destroy us."

"Just because a war monitor . . ."

"They mean to destroy us. I assure you of this."

"What makes you think that?"

Director Tchung stared over Sil-Chan's head at an empty space above the fandoor. *So impatient! When I was his age I already was married and with two children. How can Records name Sil-Chan as my most logical successor? A man re-*

quires familial stability for this position.

"There is no doubt whatsoever about my assessment of our peril," Tchung said.

The wordy old fool!

Sil-Chan hitched himself forward in his chair. "But how . . ."

"One of our random broadcasts reviewed an ancient play of the Trosair period. It was a humorous review, in fact very amusing—a farce. It poked fun at an imaginary government called The Myrmidion Enclave."

Sil-Chan felt his mouth go dry. "Myrmidion. . . ."

"Indeed—a cosmic jest. Coincidence? Tell that to our government. Tell that to Supreme Imperator Hobart of Myrmid. Tell it to the Myrmid Enclave."

"It has to be a coincidence," Sil-Chan said. "We'll show them how the random selection system works. No one interferes with that. We'll . . ."

"The accountants come directly from Hobart of Myrmid. Our own Records section, the Central Computer—all agree that the accountants have orders to destroy us."

"Then we'll fight!"

"We will not fight!" Tchung sank back into his chair, breathing heavily. "At least, we will not offer them violence."

"Then let's send out collection ships to enlist help for . . ."

"The accountants have already requisitioned every gram of fuel wire on the planet. Our ships are grounded."

"They can't do that! We . . ."

"They are the government," Tchung reminded him. "And we obey the government."

Sil-Chan stared at the curios behind the Director. No more collection ships going out? No more additions to the Archives?

"I suppose our great age is against us," Tchung said. "We've existed so long, it was inevitable that one day we would have to cope with . . . with coincidence."

"Perhaps if we seceded from . . ."

"Hah!" Tchung glowered at his subordinate. "And us a hollow ball of storage space full of records and artifacts! We're completely dependent upon Galactic subsidy. We've nothing to draw upon to support ourselves or to fuel our collection ships. We've only one commodity— the stored knowledge and information. We're mankind's memory. It has suddenly been rediscovered that certain memories can be dangerous."

"What can we . . ."

"Not we, you." Tchung pointed a finger at him. "You can anticipate that snooping accountant staff. You must justify every expenditure, every credit that we . . ."

"Sir? Nothing I do can justify us if they don't want to accept our arguments."

Tchung drew in a deep breath, exhaled slowly. "Yes, of course. But the government accountants are inquiring into the Dornbaker Account. I want . . ."

"Dornbaker Account?" Sil-Chan stared in puzzlement at the Director.

"Yes, the Dornbaker Account. I summoned you because the discrepancies are enormous. I want you to . . ."

"I've never heard of a Dornbaker Account."

Tchung stared at him. "But you're the Chief Accountant!"

"I know, sir, but . . ."

"Wait." Tchung reached into the message chute behind his desk, retrieved a thick sheaf of inter-Library micros and fed them into the player above the chute. "I asked for the actual material when it . . . I mean, I didn't want this playing over any of our internal circuits."

"If it's sensitive, I can understand the secrecy, sir. But that's quite a package. All of that in one account?"

"It's a condensation, Sooma. A condensation."

"But why . . . I mean, if I'm to shepherd these accountants around and . . . Sir, I've never

heard of this Dornbaker Account. I swear it. What is it?''

Tchung nodded. "I suspected that. You understand that I do not mistrust your competency. But I was naturally worried about the activities of these. . . . as you say, jackals. I thought I would look into the larger expenses, find what . . ."

"That's the very thing I've been doing, sir. I have my people poring over everything."

"Not quite everything. You see, I requested the records on all large expenses of long standing that have not been reviewed or readjusted for several centuries."

Tchung cleared his throat.

"So?"

"I . . . uh . . . turned over the preliminary examination to an assistant. He was distracted for a few days over the costs in the sub-micro refiling system. We all know *that's* top priority if we ever hope to effect any big savings in . . . Oh, dear. I'm explaining this badly."

"What did your assistant find?"

"The Dornbaker Account. For three days we have been receiving nothing but material on this Dornbaker Account."

"One account?"

"That's why I was so sure that my Chief Accountant would know what . . ."

Sil-Chan pressed backward into his chair.

"Impossible! There's no account in our records that big."

"I'm afraid there's at least one such account. Material on it is still pouring out. The last running tab showed eighteen billion stellars spent on the Dornbaker Account in the first seven months of this fiscal year."

Sil-Chan opened his mouth, closed it without a word. Then: "I shall resign immediately, of course. I cannot . . ."

"Oh, don't be a fool! Not a complete fool, at least."

"Sir, I don't understand how you got these records and we in Accountancy have never heard of them."

"It was the way I phrased my request. How do you summon the records each year?"

"Accounts for readjustment, of course."

"I asked for *all* large expenses."

Sil-Chan crimsoned.

"Don't blame yourself, my boy," Tchung said. "I know the procedure. How could you suspect such a . . ."

"Even so, our cross-checks and random accounting procedures . . . anything that big has to be justified in the budgets!"

"It was marked DA. Does that suggest anything to you?"

"Deteriorated Accumulation—the fuel budget!

Deteriorated fuel. I see! It was . . ."

" . . . thrown in with fuel costs. They were large, but we expect them to be large and. . . ."

"Doesn't the Central Computer explain this Dornbaker Account?"

Tchung referred to the micro projection on his desk, flipped switches and read from the projection. "It refers to Dornbaker access, Dornbaker counterbalance —that's one million six hundred and eight thousand stellars annually just for robot upkeep—and there's Dornbaker re-routing and . . ." Tchung mopped his forehead. "It takes forty-two minutes just to list the subsections of this account. I won't go on with it."

Sil-Chan swallowed in a dry throat. "Forty-two minutes just to . . . Did you say *counterbalance?*"

"Yes."

"There's obviously some stupid error here, sir. How could. . . ."

"No error. When I saw *counterbalance,* I began to suspect that . . . well . . . You must understand, Sooma, that some matters are reserved for the Director. There's a question of legality here. It seems that we don't have the legal right to read-just this account."

"But all that money, sir. How long since that account has even been studied for possible . . ."

"Five thousand and two Standard Years Modern, six thousand and twenty-nine by the old reckoning."

Sil-Chan felt a constriction of his chest. He felt suddenly old and incomplete. "I know, sir, that we've never been noted for our economies, but. . . ."

Tchung waved him to silence. "I will risk the open channels." He flipped a switch beside his desk projector, indicated the open microphone to the Central Computer. "Sooma, how would you phrase the question to get as succinct an answer as possible? Seventy-four point four one two percent of standby and primary logic banks already are engaged in the first phase of this Dornbaker Account. You must ask a question which uses a primary channel without higher monitor."

Sil-Chan nodded, ran a hand through his blonde brush. "Computer?"

"Computer recognizes Sil-Chan." The metallic voice carried an impersonal and attenuated tone which Sil-Chan found uncharacteristic. Perhaps it was Tchung's own office setting.

"I am propounding a top priority question," Sil-Chan said. "This question takes precedence over all other matters now being considered. Give us an elementary, condensed explanation which requires no more than a few minutes—What is this Dornbaker Account?"

A rasping buzz sounded from the speaker fol-

lowed by clicks and tappings, then the metallic voice: "Information available only to the Director."

"Give us that information!" Tchung ordered.

"Computer recognizes Director Tchung," the metallic voice said. "Does Director Tchung wish this information disclosed to the other person with him?"

"Yes!"

"Noted and filed. Free Island Dornbaker is a land mass of approximately two hundred and seventy-four kilometers length, one hundred and fifty-eight kilometers width. It is located on planet surface approximately four hundred kilometers from the community of Magsayan which is on the shores of Climatic Control Sea number fifteen. The island. . . ."

"Island?" Sil-Chan interrupted.

"A body of land entirely surrounded by water," said the computer."

"I know what an island is!" Sil-Chan snapped. "I was just surprised."

"Computer cannot always distinguish between surprise and the need to know," the Computer said.

"Get on with it!" Tchung ordered.

"Dornbaker Free Island is an autonomous area by treaty and numerous precedental decisions in Stellar Law that would be applicable in present

circumstances. Beneath the island in roughly a cone shape, the original property attached to the autonomous area projects to within three hundred kilometers of planetary core. There is also the restriction on airspace which . . ."

"Under the island?" Sil-Chan asked.

Tchung nodded.

The Computer clicked, then: "Surprise or interrogation?"

"Interrogation," Sil-Chan said.

"Computer obeys. The three hundred kilometers beneath this downward projection were ceded to Galactic Archives when this planet was the Terran Autonomy. That was at the time of the gravitronic unit's installation. This installation occurred immediately prior to the planetary reduction in mass which made room for storage of . . ."

"But what do you mean by cone-shaped property?" Sil-Chan demanded.

"That portion of Old Terra within the autonomous boundaries of the Free Island and projecting downward toward this planet's true core."

Sil-Chan stared across the desk at Tchung. "Does the Computer mean . . . Earth?"

The Computer responded ahead of Tchung: "That is the most common referent, but actually most of it is solidified magmas.

"Then the counterbalance . . ." Sil-Chan said.

"The counterbalance," the Computer explained, "is required to counteract the tremendous weight differential created by the autonomous mass upon the southern equatorial belt. If that weight were permitted to change the planetary axis and . . ."

Sil-Chan interrupted: "This thing is saying that there's a gigantic mass of Old Terra under some island and projecting almost to the planet's core."

The Computer said: "Correct restatement."

"How could we miss such a thing?" Sil-Chan asked. "It must be monstrous. Why the . . ." He broke off and shook his head.

The Computer said: "Does Sil-Chan wish a psychological explanation, or one derived from probabilities based on the physical limits of . . ."

"Are there people on that island?" Sil-Chan asked.

The Computer said: "The island is occupied by Clan Dornbaker and related groups—Coogans, Atvards . . ."

"There is even a Tchung branch on the island," the Director said.

Sil-Chan chewed his lips. How much did the Director really know?

"Do you wish a continued listing?" the Computer asked.

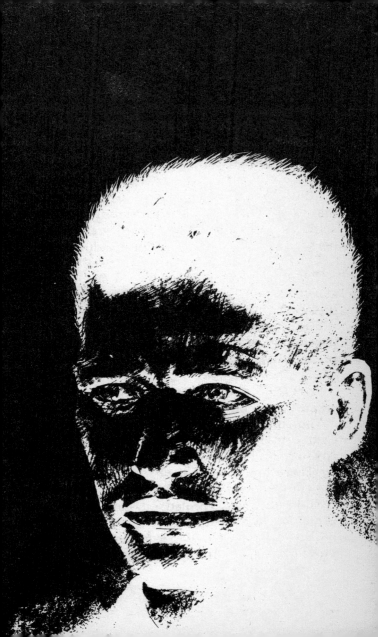

"How are they governed?" Sil-Chan asked.

"The hereditary ruler of Free Island, always a Dornbaker by name and blood, is called the Paternomer. The Paternomer's powers are tempered by several factors—a Council of Elders, something called 'an appeal to the Pleb' and various religious considerations. Computer's auto-sensories do not extend into the autonomous area, but evidence has accumulated over the centuries. The present population, stabilized at about three thousand persons, appears to work for a common idyllic vision of. . . ."

"You spoke of religious considerations," Sil-Chan said.

"The inhabitants give obeisance to 'The Book of Stone.' That is a Middle-Era translation of an ancient work from Old Terra which revolves around a leader called 'The Rock.' "

"I know that one," Sil-Chan said. "What I don't understand is how we could have overlooked this thing if it projects right down into the planet that way."

The Computer took this as another question. "Most auditing is automatic. The physical appearance of interior walls which confine Free Island's downward projection cannot be differentiated from normal Archives walls. Flights over the island without permission are prohibited in the original treaty. All flight lanes, therefore, automatically bypass Free Island. There are also other factors—deeper and psychological which go into . . ."

"Let's get the Dornbakers to cede their blasted projection and have done with it," Sil-Chan said. "We can't fight a government economy drive while a thing like that is draining us. If those government accountants even get wind of this, we're. . . ."

"There can be no question of them ceding," Tchung said.

"You're still the Director," Sil-Chan said. "The Library is the planet, the planet is the Library. You're the boss."

"Certain services and credits were agreed upon in the original treaty," Tchung said. "Computer, explain the accounts payable and the services."

"Services continue with internal cost readjustments. The credits to the Dornbakers have been accruing unclaimed and without readjustment for more than four thousand periods."

His voice hoarse, Sil-Chan asked: "How much do we owe them?"

"The full sum is not an intelligible figure," the Computer said. "That much currency does not exist in the known universe."

"Could they demand payment?" Sil-Chan whispered.

"It would be legal," the Computer said.

"Then they own us!"

"Technically, that is true," the Computer said. "However, no such action by Clan Dornbaker has been taken nor is it anticipated."

"Is there a legal way to take that island or its downward projection from the Dornbakers?" Sil-Chan asked.

Tchung smiled and closed his eyes.

The Computer clicked rhythmically for almost a minute, then: "You cannot take the island legally. Some compromise may be possible. It should be considered that the Dornbakers do not know about their legal position. Much time has passed since the treaty. They apparently live a primitive life on the island. One possible approach occurs: Free Island is a sanctuary for a large tree called Sequoia Gigantica. These trees require a rather delicate weather balance. Dornbakers nurture a superstition that 'As long as the Sequoia stand the Free Island shall remain free.' "

"Not the trees," Tchung said. "We will not threaten the trees."

"Weather control specifications in the original treaty are, however, open to different interpretations," the Computer said.

"Not the trees and that's final," Tchung said.

Sil-Chan had never heard such force in

Tchung's voice. The old man appeared suddenly hard and decisive—a characteristic Sil-Chan had never before detected.

"What . . . what can we do?" Sil-Chan asked. He felt that he had been cut loose from his roots. His career, his work—his dream to sit one day in Tchung's chair—all were floating away from him.

"I will arrange for you to take a private jetter and ago alone to the Free Island," Tchung said. "Find out how we can use that island to free ourselves from the grip of this Myrmid government and it's damnable accountants."

"Use . . ." Sil-Chan shook his head. "Sir, if they get the slightest hint that we're in this fix, the Dornbakers may join our enemies."

"There is that possibility," Tchung said. "I trust, however, that you can avoid it. There is no time to lose. I suggest you get going."

Sil-Chan wet his lips with his tongue. "Do I . . . Shouldn't I gather more information about. . . ."

"There's no better source of the information than the Free Island itself," Tchung said. "Report to me on a scrambled channel."

Sil-Chan arose. He felt that he had been maneuvered into an impossible situation. His devotion to the Library was well known . . . and perhaps that was why he had been chosen for this

mission. Loyalty. And he had been the Chief Accountant, the one who had never discovered this Dornbaker Account. Slowly, Sil-Chan left the office. Guilt and Loyalty confused him. They did not seem compatible but he felt himself driven by them.

After two more days of examining the Dornbaker Account, Tchung sat alone in the quiet of his office. He could sense the weight of all those honeycombed corridors above him—thousands of them—and more below. He was a mote in this system or even less, much less than a mote. And in the immensity of the universe, even this planet with its precious contents dwindled to insignificance.

A glance at his chrono showed it to be late afternoon topside. Sil-Chan already would be on the Free Island. Tchung looked at the projector with its explosive figures. *Climate Control: sixty-six thousand stellars monthly! Aih! He rubbed at his temples. It is I who have failed, not poor Sil-Chan.*

A deep sigh shook the Director. *What if I have made another mistake?* But the young man was unmarried and handsome—virile. Records said he took anti-S to suppress his normal sexual drive and to free his energies for service to the Library. A very strange young man.

Abruptly, the autosecretary shattered his reverie with its metallic compuer voice: "Ser Perlig Ambroso, chief government accountant, to see Archives Director Tchung."

Tchung pushed the release button for his fandoor. The fans slammed open and Ambroso burst into the room as though released from a spring. He was a round-cheeked, florid man with sandy hair—the flesh of a once-active man who was now gaining fat instead of muscle. A winebibber, the reports said. His eyes were small, blue and hard and he spoke in the flat voice of command. Ambroso had presented a front of good humor at their first meeting. No such front covered him now.

"Tchung!" he spat. "Are you deliberately impeding us?"

"I . . . of course not!" Tchung stared up at his accuser. That sharp manner. Ambroso was a military man!

"Your computer reacts like a pregnant swert in a drogo swamp," Ambroso said. He leaned baby-wrinkled knuckles on Tchung's desk. "When I demand to know why, I am informed that more than three-fourths of your circuits are engaged on a problem to which your staff has assigned top priority. Explain."

Tchung swallowed. *The Dornbaker Account! Oh, Holy Director of Heavenly Archives! If I open*

*those circuits, these government jackals may go
directly to the Dornbaker Account.*

"What are those circuits doing?" Ambroso
demanded.

Tchung hesitated on the brink of an outright
lie, then the conditioning of a lifetime's devotion
to his Code took over. "They are working on the
problem of greater economy in our operations,
Ser Ambroso."

"We will take care of your economy problem-
s," Ambroso said. "You clear those circuits."

"Immediately." Tchung turned to his controls,
flipped the computer switch, said: "The government accountants working in Section CC of
the two hundred and twenty-fourth sublevel will
have top priority on all computer time. All previ-
ous priority commitments are rescinded by this
order."

The speaker emitted a curious coughing buzz,
then: "Acknowledged and filed."

Once more, Tchung looked up at Ambroso.
"Forgive us, please. It was not a deliberate
obstruction. The first rule of our Code is that we
must obey the government."

"So you say." Ambroso allowed himself a slow
smile. "But if there are further indications that
you are attempting to obstruct us, I will land a
force from the monitor to insure that there are no
recurrences."

"I'm sure that will not be necessary," Tchung said.

Again, Ambroso smiled. It was like a tic, gone almost before Tchung could be sure of it. Ambroso started to turn away, paused, his attention caught by the curios on the table behind Tchung. In four swift strides, Ambroso was at the table, lifting the golden statuette from it. The figure was of a small winged boot with a Naos inscription on the base.

"Expensive bauble," Ambroso said. "Did official funds go for this decoration?"

"A gift from the Researchers of Naos on our ten thousandth anniversary," Tchung said.

Again, the tic-smile touched Ambroso's face. He replaced the statuette delicately. "So very long. So very, very long. And all of those centuries you have beamed your nonsense into space. So many wasteful broadcasts without an iota of information."

Tchung's features stiffened. "We broadcast many things, that is true. Our information has a varied value. Program selection is, as you know, purely random. Our charter assumes a mathematical probability that significant data will be selected every. . . ."

"Yes, yes," Ambroso said. "So it's claimed."

"Concepts of value differ," Tchung said. "That does not alter the fact that we gather artifacts and

information from the far reaches of our universe . . . and that we hold back nothing in what we disseminate."

"Too much rubble to wade through for the occasional gem," Ambroso said. "Your gems come to be more and more unexpected."

Tchung concealed his anger and murmured: "It has been said that we deal in the unexpected. But there are times when the unexpected can be devastating."

"As devastating as the weapons on our monitor?" Ambroso asked.

"Ours are not the ways of violence," Tchung said.

"And times change," Ambroso said. "New ways clear out the errors of the past. They make way for . . ."

"The errors of the future," Tchung said.

Ambroso glowered at him. "You collect useless junk! Pack Rats!"

"They once were known as Trade Rats," Tchung said. "The original animals, I mean. They stole from campers in the wilderness, and always left something behind from the nest. That Trade Rat nest might contain a ruby which would be traded for a small piece of elastic. Fortunate the camper when that happened."

"What about the camper who lost a ruby and got a small bit of elastic?" Ambroso asked. He grinned at Tchung, whirled away and strode from the office.

When the fandoors closed, Tchung picked up the winged boot, rubbed it with his thumb. The Naos Researchers had been particularly grateful. Archives had saved them three centuries of work on the problem of random-desire adjustment in conflicting human groups. The Naos planets were known today for the dynamic spirit of their people, a fact recorded in the inscription beneath the golden boot:

"Information is the tool and the goad of intelligence."

Tchung replaced the winged boot on the shelf. The thing had filled him with a momentary sense of the hoary antiquity over which he presided—a sense he had not experienced in quite that way since his youth. This was followed immediately by a nostalgia which tightened his throat.

Is it about to end?

Unconsciously, he turned in the direction of Free Island Dornbaker. *Your secret is out, but the stakes are higher than anyone anticipated. Act wisely, Sil-Chan . . . but not too wisely.*

Sil-Chan had approached Free Island Dornbaker at mid-morning, his hands on the jetter's controls slippery with perspiration. He found himself in the grip of an illogical desire to turn

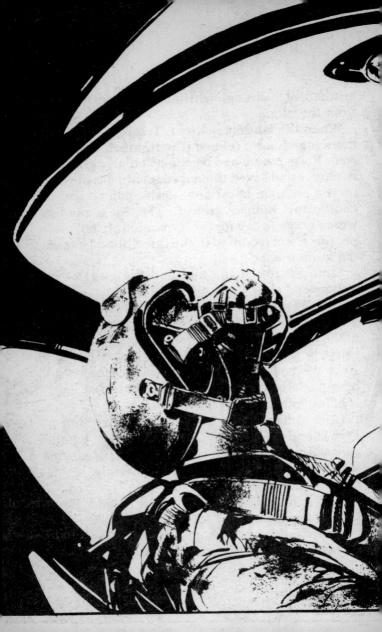

and run. The closer he came to the island, the greater this feeling became.

There had been nerve-straining delays at Magsayan while officials cleared his flight to the island. The officials had professed surprise that an island lay out there in the misty sea, although they had cleared flights around the area all of their professional lives. Sil-Chan had provided them with a special channel code, however, and a voice-only communication had ensued, someone out there identified as Free Island Control being very obstructive and then, unexplainably helpful.

Sil-Chan kept his equipment tuned to the Free Island channel while he winged over the sea. The island was growing more distinct by the minute, emerging from silvery mists. He saw steeply wooded hills, the flashing blue of streams, rare white dots of buildings half hidden in greenery. White surf frothed the coastline.

The place looked wild . . . un-Terran—not at all like the familiar rolling contours of the park-like mainland. He emerged from the last of the mists into sunlight and more details impressed themselves upon him. Sil-Chan gasped. What had appeared from a distance to be steep hills covered with mossy scrub was actually ranks of gigantic trees. They speared the sky. Monstrous trees!

His speaker burped, crackled and a feminine voice came on: "This is Free Island Control calling the jetter."

Sil-Chan punched his transmit button: "This is the jetter."

The feminine voice said: "We have you on longshot. You are approaching on isthmus and bay. At the head of the bay you will see a line of low white buildings. Turn inland directly over them. Come down close. You want to be no more than fifty meters above the ridge behind those buildings when you cross it."

"Fifty meters, right." Sil-Chan tuned his altimeter.

The feminine voice continued: "Just over that hill we've mowed an east-west landing strip for you. If you line up over the white buildings and stay low, you should . . ."

"Mowed?" Sil-Chan blurted the word with his finger pressed hard on transmit.

The feminine voice paused, then: "Yes, mowed. You should've taken a copter instead of that hot jobby. I was about to suggest it when the PN said he would like to see one of the new jetters."

Sil-Chan tried to swallow past a thickness in his throat. "I see the white buildings. There are three of them. I am turning."

"Fifty meters, no more."

Sil-Chan checked his crash harness. "Right."

"Do you see one taller tree on the hill?"

"Yes."

"As low as possible over that tree. Dip into the valley beyond. Line up with the flagpole at the far end of the mowed field. Stay right down the middle and you'll miss the tall grass. I sure hope the strip's long enough."

So do I, Sil-Chan thought.

The tall tree loomed ahead. He lifted slightly, then dipped and gasped as he saw the tiny field. There was time only for a blurred glimpse of flagpole, trees beyond and a mist-colored cliff rising abruptly right behind the trees. No time to swerve or climb out. He kicked on full flaps, fired the rocket idiot-brakes in the nose and fought to hold control as the ship bucked down into dangerous low speed.

A path of darker green lay down the middle of the lighter green field. He aimed into the center, slammed on the wheel brakes when he felt the ground. The jetter bounced up onto its nose wheel, skidded in the slippery grass, crabbed sideways into tall grass. One wing dipped. The ship cartwheeled—once, twice.

It came to rest upside down.

Sil-Chan hung in his harness trying to breathe deeply while his mind replayed the whirling madcap landscape through which he had just dervished. He felt his heart pounding. His left shoulder ached.

That cost me half my longevity.

The adrenaline reaction began to set in. His hands trembled uncontrollably. He knew he would have to find a supply of anti-S soon. That dive had taken him through months of normal life.

The jetter creaked and settled slightly. A strange quiet intruded upon Sil-Chan's awareness. The quiet bothered him. Faint swishing grew discernible. A masculine voice intruded on the quiet.

"Hey in there! You all right?"

Sil-Chan could imagine the racing stream of robot emergency equipment which would have greeted such a landing on a regular field. He shuddered. All of the quiet, single-purposed reserve which had marked his life to this point disolved like the mists around the island. It was as though he had passed through an invisible barrier to become an unexpected person on the other side.

"You funnel-mouthed, vacuum-headed idiots!" he bellowed.

The jetter trembled as someone forced open the door beside him. He turned his head, looked upside down into the face of a man who reminded him of a younger Director Tchung. It was the set

of the eyes and the reserved look in a narrow face.

"You sound healthy enough," the man said. "Did you break anything?"

"No thanks to you!" Sil-Chan raged.

"Here, let me help you out of the harness," the man said. He knelt and gently helped Sil-Chan remove the crash harness. The man's hands were rough and there was unexpected strength in his arms. He smelled of some odd spice.

Sil-Chan winced as the straps were eased over his left shoulder.

"Bit of a bruise there," the man said. "Doesn't feel like anything's broken. How about your legs and back?"

"They're fine. Get me out of this stupid . . ."

"Easy there. Easy does it."

The man gentled Sil-Chan out the door and onto the grassy ground, helped Sil-Chan to sit up. There was an acrid fuel smell mixed with the odors of crushed grass. The sky swayed a bit above his rescuer.

"Just sit there a bit until you feel better," the man said. "You seem to be all in one piece."

Sil-Chan studied this first Dornbaker he had seen. The man was a loosely hung figure in a brown fringed jacket, tight pants. The jacket was open almost to his navel and exposed a smooth, almost hairless chest. The same could not be said of his head—which was a tangle of black hair,

some of which straggled over his forehead, He looked as primitive and wild as this island.

"David! David! Is he all right?"

It was the voice of the young woman at Free Island Control. She came panting around the end of the wrecked jetter, bare legs swishing in the long grass. At sight of Sil-Chan, she came to a stop and leaned against the jetter, gasping for breath. "Thank the Stone you weren't killed," she panted. "I ran all the way from Control."

Sil-Chan stared up at her: skin as dark as Tchung's but her hair was a golden cloud and her eyes were the blue of the misty sea, full of lurking merriment that even her obvious worry could not conceal. She, too, wore the oddly fringed clothing, but a curve of bright red blouse filled the wedge of her jacket. It came to Sil-Chan that she was the most delicately beautiful creature he had ever seen. He found himself unable to look away from that lovely face, the soft mouth, the tiny nose, the smooth rounding of chin and cheeks. All of the careful repression that had kept him grinning upward in the Archival hierarchy, everything of his past peeled away. It was an effort to wrench himself back to duty. He cleared his throat.

Before he could speak, she said: "I told them that runway was too short. But no! They had to get off right away on the hunt!"

"Easy, Hep," the man said. His voice floated out in an effortless baritone.

Sil-Chan shook his head to clear it of that lovely female vision. "Would you direct me to the Paternomer, please?" he asked.

"He won't be back for two days," the man aid. "I'm David. This is Hepzebah." He spoke the names as though they should convey important information. "We're to take care of you until the PN returns."

Stiffly, painfully, Sil-Chan levered himself to his feet, waving away David's profered help. "I have to see the Paternomer as soon as possible. Can you take me to him?" He glanced at the wreck. "This hardly seems the way to get to him anymore."

"We're very sorry about that," Hepzebah said. "Really, we had nothing to do with the arrangements."

"I'm afraid you'll have to wait for the PN's return," David said. "No way to get to him when he's on a hunt."

"But it's urgent and I . . ."

"You sure aren't going back mainland in that." Hepzebah indicated the wreck. "Best you stay. My brother here has tight quarters and he's a good host when he wants to be."

Brother!

Once more, Sil-Chan found himself staring at

Hepzebah. *Lovely. Lovely. And such a charming name.* There was a painful constriction in his chest where the crash harness could not have touched him. *Brother.* Sil-Chan had feared they might be a mated pair. She still might have a mate somewhere.

She blushed under the steadiness of his stare. *I mustn't stare. I must say something.*

"It's a very nice day," he said.

"Yes, it is," she agreed. "Let's go over to David's." She waved at a low structure in the trees at the side of the field. Sil-Chan had not noticed it until she pointed, as though she had created the structure by some wild magic—red-brown logs, rock chimney, small windows. It nestled among the trees as though it has grown there.

"You're favoring your left arm," David said. "We'd best go in and have a look at it." He turned and led the way across the tall grass.

Sil-Chan kept pace behind with Hepzebah walking close beside, studying him. There was a penetrating quality to her stare which made Sil-Chan uncomfortable but he would not have had her look away for anything. *Lovely!* "I'm sorry I blew up back there," he said.

"You had a perfect right," she said. "I'd have never permitted it, but the PN makes all his own rules. He sent us in from Big North Cape to greet you and didn't give us enough help. They wouldn't make other arrangements—only what the PN ordered."

"There was the hunt," David said. He spoke without turning.

"The hunt!" she flared. "You're here because you're the Aitch/Aye." She turned to Sil-Chan. "David has to do all the official work that the PN doesn't want to do. The PN made me come because I wouldn't take the trothing. He thinks he's punishing me."

Sil-Chan shook his head. What were they talking about? He said: "I'm afraid I don't understand."

"He's from far mainland," David said. "You're making no sense to him." David slowed his pace and walked beside Hepzebah, speaking across her to explain. "Hep wouldn't accept the mate the brothers picked for her. Made the PN angry. She really doesn't have to accept, but the PN's K-cousins are expected to obey. Things are different with H- and B-cousins."

Sil-Chan stared back at David without comprehension.

"No sense yourself!" Hepzebah laughed.

"Is it some special language?" Sil-Chan asked.

David grinned. They were into the trees now, within only a few steps of a wide split-wood door into the house.

"It's Dornbakerish, I guess," David said. I'll try again. I was tolled off to greet you because the PN wouldn't miss the hunt. He's getting old and he figures he doesn't have many more. They're running fallow deer on Big Plain. That's why I'm here. I'm the Aitch Aye. That means I'll be PN when the present PN goes upStone. Hep's of the same line, a K-cousin. She . . ."

"What is a K-cousin?" Sil-Chan asked.

They stopped just outside the wide door of the house.

David looked at Hepzebah. She looked at David. Presently, she looked at Sil-Chan. "Just K-cousin," she said. "It's close. I'm of the PN's line. One of my boy-children will be picked to succeed David."

"You . . . have children?" Sil-Chan asked.

"Oh, no. I don't even have a mate. And the PN's angry at me, punishing . . ."

"The PN isn't that petty," David said. He opened the door, exposed a dim interior into which he motioned Sil-Chan. "My honored guest, Sooma Sil-Chan. Enter my abode and call it your own."

"You know my name?"

"David signed the clearance for the PN," Hepzebah said. She followed Sil-Chan into the house.

David brought up the rear and closed the door.

Sil-Chan stared at the room—long with a ceiling which reached away to dim rafters. Windows looked out onto the landing field and the wrecked jetter . . . more windows peered into shadowy woods . . . gigantic rock fireplace at one end, smoke blackened. There was a smell of smoke in the room. Odd projections on the walls. Sil-Chan peered at them, realized they were the mounted heads of horned animals. There was a small fire in the fireplace. David crossed to it, stirred up the falame and added more logs.

Hepzebah touched Sil-Chan's arm, said: "Come over by the fire and let me look at your shoulder. David, get a refresher, a good stiff one."

"Right." David walked off toward a door opposite the fireplace.

Sil-Chan's mind reeled. This entrancing woman was not wed! David was Aitch Aye. What was that? Sil-Chan felt that he had read of such a relationship somewhere in the Library. *Heir Apparent! Yes, of course.* And Hepzebah was 'of the same line.' Gods of the universe! This pair was royalty!

"Come along," Hepzebah said.

Sil-Chan allowed himself to be led to a low-backed divan beside the fireplace. Flames murmured in the logs. The smell of smoke was stronger here. He stumbled over something that rang musically.

"One of the children left a toy," Hepzebah said. "David's so easy with them." She indicated the divan. "Sit down and take off your jacket. I'll . . ."

"No, really. It's all right," Sil-Chan said. Again, he found himself trapped in her eyes—the soft look of them here in the shadowed room . . . like some forest animal. *She's not wedded. She's not wedded.*

"I'll have a look all the same," she said. She put a light pressure on his shoulder and he sank to the divan. It was soft, absorbing and smelled of animal.

Hepzebah bent over him, and Sil-Chan inhaled a mind-rolling musk of perfumed hair. He allowed her to help him out of his jacket and shirt. The jacket was torn at the elbow and he had not even noticed. His flesh tingled where Hepzebah touched him.

"Bad bruise on your shoulder and a scratch above your left elbow," she said. She went to a door beside the fireplace, returned in a moment with a cloth which smelled of ungent. The cloth felt cool and soothing where she pressed it to his shoulder.

"What's a trothing?" Sil-Chan asked.

"The trothers are the clan elders. They decide if a joining will be good for the clan."

He swallowed. "Do you ever . . . wed outside

your clan?"

She lowered her eyes. "Sometimes."

Sil-Chan studied the soft oval of her face, imagined that face pillowed beside him. His mission, the Archive's problems, Tchung—all melted into the distance . . . another planet.

"Drink this."

It was Davis suddenly standing behind him, proferring an earthen mug that swirled with pungent brown liquid and a biting aroma. Sil-Chan tasted it: hot, tangy and sharp on the tongue. He downed the drink. Warmth filled him. He re-experienced the inner release he had felt after crashing the jetter—another person. He stood up.

"How does one arrange a troth?" he asked.

She peered up at him, a smile touching her lips. Something smokey and wondering drifted in her eyes. "We have several ways. The PN's K-cousins can take the initiative if the couple ask it."

"What's all this talk of trothing?" David asked. He came around the divan and stood with his back to the fire.

Hepzebah waved a hand in front of Sil-Chan's eyes, leaned close to stare at him.

Sil-Chan said: "What're you. . . ."

"I have the inward eye," she said. "You go very deep. It's warm and nice in there."

David said: "I asked you . . ."

"If he'll have me, David, I'm going to open the troth," she said.

David looked at Sil-Chan, at Hepzebah. "I haven't been out of the room *that* long, have I? I just went for a drink."

She touched Sil-Chan tentatively on the wrist. Again, he felt his flesh tingle.

"This is nonsense," David said.

Her hand stole into Sil-Chan's. He felt the perfect fit of her there, the perfection of her beside him.

"Will you wed me, Sooma Sil-Chan?" she asked.

"Hep, you stop this!" David said.

"Be quiet, David," she said, "or I will tell stories about a young man's secret visits to the mainland."

"Now, Hep! You . . ."

"Quiet, I said."

Sil-Chan felt himself bathed in a warm glow—the drink inside him, Hepzebah's hand in his. *Wed her?*

"I'd go to the ends of the universe to wed you," he whispered.

"Is that a yes?" she asked.

"Yes. Yes."

"But you've only just met!" David protested.

"The trothers will agree with me," she said.

"But I already know. The inward eye never fails."
She tipped her head, looked up at Sil-Chan from
the corners of her eyes. "I find him very attrac-
tive."

David appeared angry. "He's just different."

"I'm already certain," she said. "And you
heard the question and you heard his response."

"This is too much!" David raged. "You're always doing things like this!"

Sil-Chan experienced a crawling of goose
flesh. He felt delirious. All those years of celibacy
and devotion to duty and career had melted
away.

"He'll never take the name!" David said. "Just
to look at him you can tell. You'd best accept
Martin as the trothers . . ."

"Gun the trothers!" Steel in her voice. "So if he
won't take the name, I'll go with him . . . as is
right. We'll cross that river when it cuts our
trail."

"This is much too quick," David said. "The PN
will blast the roof off when he . . ."

"His sister's son and your sister's son—that's
the way of the PN," she said. "Let us never forget
it."

When he responded, David's voice was lower.
"Still too quick."

Sil-Chan looked from one to the other. He took
strength from the feeling of Hepzebah's hand in

his. There was no need for logic or reason.

"I've always been a quick one," Hepzebah said. "I make decisions the way the ice breaks from the glacier."

David threw up his hands.

"This is impossible. You're impossible!"

"When will we wed?" Sil-Chan asked.

"A month," she said. "That we cannot speed."

David said: "Hep, if you would just . . ."

"I warned you, David."

David turned to Sil-Chan. "Do you have any idea of what you're starting?"

The question ran a finger of ice down Sil-Chan's spine. He was here to negotiate with the Paternoster. What happened to that if the PN were alienated at the start?

"I knew it would be a day of turning," Hepzebah said. "A flight of plover settled in the grass outside my window at dawn. One remained when the others flew on. It called to me before following the flight."

"The PN will blow down the trees," David said. "He wants Hep to wed Martin. Joining the two lines will prevent disputes." He whirled on Hepzebah. "You know that!"

"There are others to do the joining," she said. "It will be done."

David flicked a glance at Sil-Chan. "What if this one changes . . ."

"Have I ever been wrong, David . . . about such as this?"

"The line of the PN is more important than you or anything else," David said.

"And I will join what I will join," she said.

David turned his back on her, stared into the fire. "You!" he muttered.

Tchung awoke in the black darkness of his bedroom and was several heartbeats orienting himself. The nightmare persisted in his mind. A dream of horrible reality: Ambroso had come into the Director's office, flourishing deadly weapons and laughing with the laugh of Sooma Sil-Chan. Slowly, the flesh of Ambroso had peeled away, leaving Sil-Chan who continued to laugh and flourish the weapons.

"Now you know me," the dream Sil-Chan said. "Now I am director. Be gone, old man."

"Are you awake, Pat?" It was Madame Tchung from the other bed.

Tchung was glad she could not see his perspiring face.

"Yes."

"Are you troubled, dear?"

"I'm worried about Sooma. Not a word from him."

"He'll call when he has news, dear."

"That's what I'm afraid of."

"Why is that?"

"Ambroso demanded all of my private scrambler codes today."

"And you gave them to him?"

"What else could I do. I must obey."

"That stupid rule!"

Tchung sighed.

"Sooma will find a solution," Madame Tchung said. "Records cannot have made a mistake about him."

"But he's . . . so intense."

"He's still young, dear."

"And so intense."

"Sooma had to work hard to get where he is, dear. Trust him."

Tchung sighed. "I'm trying. But it is difficult. When I was his age I was already . . ."

"You were precocious, dear. Now come over here and let me soothe you."

Sil-Chan, too, experienced a nightmare. He had been quartered by David Dornbaker in a small upper room above the fireplace "because it gets cold here at night." The cot was slender and firm, the blankets rough and smelling of animal fur. There was no pillow, and Sil-Chan's shoulder throbbed. He rolled up his clothing for a pillow and tried to sleep.

The nightmare invaded his mind.

Paternomer Dornbaker stood over him. The PN was twice the height of a normal man and his fingers ended in claws. The blood of fallow deer dripped from the claws.

"I will hunt you!" the PN raged. Clawed hands came up to threaten Sil-Chan.

Hepzebah darted in front of him. Fangs protruded from her soft mouth. "He is mine," she said an her voice was the voice of a hunter-cat. "I will drink your blood before I let you harm him."

Sil-Chan found that his arms were bound, his feet encased in tight sacking. He could not move. His voice would not obey him.

The PN moved to the left. Hepzebah darted to intercept him. The PN moved to the right. Again, Hepzebah blocked his way.

"I will drop this fool down the deepest shaft of the Library," the PN said. "Who can stop me? The Library is mine . . . mine . . . mine . . . mine. . . ."

Sil-Chan awoke to find his body encased tightly in the blankets which he had twisted around himself. His shoulder ached. Slowly, Sil-Chan freed himself from the blankets and at up on the edge of his cot. The floor was cold beneath his bare feet. There was moonglow through a tiny skylight. Shadows from the limbs of giant trees painted images on the floor.

Tomorrow, he and Hepzebah would have a day

to themselves. The PN would arrive on the following day.

What can I tell him?

Sil-Chan felt that he had been enchanted, caught in a magic web. *I know it and I don't care.* What matter the Dornbaker Account? Nothing mattered except the enchantment.

But I can't abandon the Library. Tchung depends on me.

Why did Tchung depend on him? The question had not occurred to Sil-Chan in quite that form. Why? Well . . . Tchung would not move without the advice of Records. That was certain. What could Records tell the Director about one Sooma Sil-Chan?

Sil-Chan looked inward at his own past life—a dedicated Library slave, little better than one of the robots. Self-programming, of course. Too single-minded for most people. Few friends. No women friends, although several had indicated more than a casual interest in him. This interest had vanished quickly when they found he was on anti-S.

Well, I'm off it now. They've probably never even heard of it on the Free Island.

He thought of Hepzebah then, conjured her face into his mind. Ahhh, with her, all things were possible.

With a sigh, Sil-Chan once more wrapped him-

self in the blankets and composed himself for sleep. This time, he invited another nightmare: His body was transformed by a witch (who looked remarkably like Hepzebah) and he became a throbbing eye which moved inward, ever deeper inward down a shaft of the Library Planet. The drop seemed endless and when it finally stopped, the eye/himself peered upward as all of the Library's contents came cascading down the shaft toward him.

"It'll blind me!" he screamed.

And he awoke to find the pale glow of morning coming through the skylight and mists drifting across the tree branches out there.

A knock sounded on his door. David's voice: "You awake?"

"Yes."

"The PN is here."

Sil-Chan sat upwright, stared at the closed door. "But he wasn't supposed to . . ."

"He's here and he wants to see you immediately. You and Hepzebah."

The Paternomer Dornbaker was not as tall as his nightmare counterpart, but he towered over Sil-Chan nonetheless. The PN stood more than two meters and his shock of grey hair added another ten centimeters. The PN was also a heavy man, muscular and swift in his movements. The early morning light penetrated the east windows to bathe the room in sharp contrasts. The PN stood out like an ancient figurehead, an older David—skin like cured leather, fan wrinkles at the corners of his eyes and mouth, a square chin, sea blue eyes and a wide mouth with dark lips.

Sil-Chan stood facing him in front of the fireplace. Hepzebah sat on the divan with David standing behind her.

The PN glared at Sil-Chan. "Why do you deliberately disrupt things of which you have no knowledge?"

Sil-Chan glanced at Hepzebah, but she was staring at the floor.

"I did not come to disrupt," Sil-Chan aid.

"I judge a man by what he does," the PN said. "How long have you been seeing my niece?"

"I met her for the first time, yesterday."

"A likely story."

"Are you calling me a liar, sir?" Sil-Chan kept his voice low and steady. It was a tone that surprised even him. The pre-Dornbaker Sil-Chan would never have used it.

The PN favored him with a peculiar, weighted stare, then: "No-o-o, I am not. But you will admit this is disruptively surprising."

"Surprising, yes."

"Why did you come here, then?"

"The Library needs your help."

"This is how you enlist my help?" He waved at Hepzebah.

She stood and moved to Sil-Chan's side, put her hand in his. "You almost killed him, Uncle, and you've not apologized."

"You stay out of this."

"Don't you take that tone with me," she said, "or I and my sisters will ban the seed. How will you find a PN then?"

He glared at her. "I'm the PN here!" He made it sound "Pen."

"And I am the Elected Womb," she said.

The PN focused on Sil-Chan. "With him?"

"With whomever I choose!"

"The trothers agreeing!"

"They'll agree."

"I'm thirsty," the PN said.

David whirled away and went into the rear of the house while the PN stared into the fire. Presently, David returned with one of the earthen mugs he had brought to Sil-Chan. The PN took the drink without looking at David, quaffed it, wiped his lips and returned the mug with the same casual disregard for its source.

"My word is law here," the PN said. "Except when I give a direct order to a chit like that." He jerked his head at Hepzebah. "You know you've interrupted my hunt?"

"David sent word to you, I know," she said.

"But you could have come back after the hunt."

"And found you already with the trothers?" He looked at Sil-Chan. "Why aren't you sitting? I told you there was no need to stand." His voice sounded suddenly old and petulant. "I know you were injured."

Sil-Chan realized that was as much of an apology as he would ever get. It amused him and strengthened him.

"You owe him something for the loss of his jetter," David ventured.

The PN whirled. "I don't owe him the woman who could join those lines! Martin's willing. Why can't she . . ."

"I have sisters," Hepzebah said. "The lines can still be joined."

"But not this year," the PN grumbled. "It's an imposition to expect an old man to wait for . . ."

Sil-Chan interrupted: "Aren't you being a little . . ."

"Stay out of this!" the PN snapped.

"I will not stay out of this!"

"You won't obey a direct order from the PN?" His voice was ominous.

Sil-Chan suppressed the churning of his stomach. "Sir, I came here at the direction of Galactic Archives, of the Library. You don't have any idea what . . ."

"We'll get to your official excuses later," the PN said. "Right now I'm trying to reason with a pig-headed female who . . ."

"Uncle." The steel had returned to Hepzebah's voice. "In front of a witness, I asked this man to wed and he accepted."

"So David says!"

"Even you are not above the law," she aid. "You will recall that I was not raised a chore daubto . . ."

"Maybe that's where I made my mistake," the PN muttered.

"If it was a mistake, it was not my mistake," she said. "And I warn you that I do not intend to be bound by your tame band o trothers when. . . ."

"You're a pig-headed female!"

She continued unperturbed. ". . . when they cast no omens, made no divinations. We both know that they followed your instructions to approve Martin."

"What's the difference? Mumbo jumbo or common sense? Give me common sense every time!" Again, he stared into the fire.

"Don't try swaying the trothers," she said. "I'll demand the Pleb. You know what'll happen then."

He spoke without turning. "Are you threatening me?"

She said: "The trothers will face the Stone and

be forced to admit your interference. The vote of the Pleb will go for me."

"All right!" He whirled. "So you want this . . . this . . ." He gestured with a fist at Sil-Chan. "Ever since you were a wee one you've gotten everything you wanted! Now you . . ."

"Will all of you shut up for just a minute?" Sil-Chan asked. "I've had quite enough of this family bickering." He caught a sudden grin from David standing behind the PN, took heart from it.

"Oh, have you now?" the PN asked. His voice was dangerous.

"I'll admit to being swept off my feet by your niece," Sil-Chan said. "Who can blame me? That's chemistry or . . . or whatever. It's wonderful and I wouldn't change it for all of Free Island. But I came here on another matter, something vital to us all."

"Do you know I could have you taken into the wilderness just like that . . ." The PN snapped his fingers. ". . . and *eliminated*, and no one the wiser."

The old Sil-Chan would have cringed at the threat. The new Sil-Chan took a step closer to the PN. "You might be able to murder me, but there'd be some the wiser!"

The PN's mouth opened, snapped shut. His chin lifted. He looked at Sil-Chan with new interest.

"We have mutual problems," Sil-Chan said. "We . . ."

"You have a talent for creating problems, no doubt of that," the PN said, but Sil-Chan senses an underlying banter in the tone.

"You may force me to return to the mainland without Hepzebah," Sil-Chan said. "But I have a mission here and I am an official of Galactic Archives."

Hepzebah squeezed Sil-Chan's hand. "If you go, I go."

The PN blinked, looked at his niece, then at Sil-Chan. "All right! What's bothering you pack rats? I want the full story."

Sil-Chan winced. Tchung's warning filled his mind. These Dornbakers could tip over the whole cart, but they might not know their legal position. So the Computer reported. Sil-Chan returned the PN's demanding stare. This was a rough man, this PN, but also a man of essential integrity . . . a man with his own code, a *wilderness honor* which might not be too different from the Library's Code. A lie would be the surest way to alienate such a man.

It occurred to Sil-Chan then that a sum which could bankrupt the government was owed to these Dornbakers. In one sense, this PN *was* the government, and the Library's Code required obedience to the government.

The PN has just ordered me to tell him the full story.

Sil-Chan did not feel that this was a line of reasoning which would stand much reconsideration, but it swayed the balance in his own mind. He began explaining about the Myrmid Enclave's jackals, the war monitor, the downward projection of Dornbaker property, the drain on Archive funds, the monstrous sum owed to the Dornbakers . . . he left out nothing.

"Why should any government acknowledge that debt?" the PN asked, when Sil-Chan had finished.

"The Enclave's jurisdiction over the planet is based on accepted responsibility. Government subsidy keeps us running, fuels the collection ships, everything. If they are not responsible for us, they have no jurisdiction here."

"In their shoes, I'd opt for a simple invasion," the PN said.

David nodded agreement. Hepzebah looked thoughtful, but did not remove her hand from Sil-Chan's.

"But the Enclave holds power through a fistful of mutual aid and defense agreements. We're not very important to that agreement—especially in a time of cost-cutting politics."

"I sympathize," the PN said, "but seems to me we could accomodate to any government. We're a simple people. Don't cost much."

"You weren't listening very well," Sil-Chan said. "You are the biggest single cost on this planet. Weather control adjustments alone take more than our robot repair budget. That's the first cost I'd cut."

"Stop our glaciers and our morning mists?" the PN asked.

"Certainly! Let you take the weather the rest of us get."

"You stop the mists and our big trees die! If they die, that sets off a chain of . . ."

"If the Enclave has its way, all services will stop . . . except perhaps the counterbalance. That'd wreck the planet."

"Do I understand you correctly?" David asked. "Free Island extends downward almost to the planet's core?"

"And upward to the edge of the atmosphere," Sil-Chan said.

"All that dirt," the PN said.

"It isn't all dirt in the strictest sense," Sil-Chan said. "Below the former magma line it's . . ."

"What's its value?" the PN asked.

"I couldn't began to tell you," Sil-Chan said.

"Seems to me," the PN mused, "our mutual problem is to make us important to that agreement which holds the government together."

"Too bad that Enclave doesn't have the Pleb,"

Hepzebah said. "If they could vote on . . ." She broke off as Sil-Chan squeezed her hand hard. He stared at her, an audacious idea taking shape in his mind.

"What's wrong?" she asked.

Sil-Chan stared at the PN. "Would you permit our technicians to install certain equipment here?"

"What equipment?"

"Technically, sir, you own this planet. But the Library is a government bureau. I doubt that you can collect, but if you demand payment that will force the convening of a new Galactic Aseembly. The Enclave *will* have to submit to a vote."

"What equipment, I say?"

"Broadcast equipment."

A speculative look spread over the PN's face. "That's pretty big trouble you'd be stirring up there, son."

"*You* would be stirring up, sir."

"How come you're calling me *sir* all of a sudden?"

"We're going to be related."

The PN grinned. "You might be getting more than you bargained for." He looked at Hepzebah. "You determined?"

"You know I am."

"Tell you one thing," the PN aid. "He won't take our name. Too much fire in him. Guess you

saw that. You asked yourself yet how the Pleb will take to a PN with another name?"

"Our child can take any name he wants," she said.

"Mayhap."

"Do we have your blessing?"

The PN frowned. "Is there one of your sisters who'll join Martin?"

"I'd try Kate. She's too young yet, but she's had her eye on that job for some time."

"Not the same as you doing it," the PN said.

"Not the same," she agreed.

The PN shook his head slowly as a faint smile turned up his lips. "By the Eternal Stone, you are a Dornbaker female!" He nodded. "My blessing to you both, then. David can tell the trothers."

Sil-Chan said: "But what about our mutual . . ."

"Oh, I'll make your broadcast," the PN said. "Always wanted to see that stuff work anyhow. Shake on it."

Sil-Chan took the proffered hand. It felt hard and calloused.

"Don't scare you very much, do I?" the PN asked.

"Not very much," Sil-Chan said.

"Good. You write out the words you want me to say. Have one of the scriveners put it in big letters for me. My eyes aren't what they were."

"Yes, sir. I will."

Abruptly, the PN turned away and strode toward the door to the outside. He jerked it open. "Now where in Stone is my Merlin? Never around when you need him!"

There was a great rodent-scurrying of human activity before David Dorbaker's fireplace. Furniture had been moved back. A thick cable reached from a metal stand across the floor to a window and trailed away outside to where the dish of a power receiver had been installed. Archives technicians were busy dismantling a temporary stand opposite the fireplace, removing one of the great broadcast adapters from the stand. The thick cable, however, remained, as did a bank of mobile rhomboids along the wall beside the fireplace. The rhomboids remained in standby mode with no realized images dancing in front of them.

Sil-Chan stood with Hepzebah looking out at the afternoon light on the mowed field where he had wrecked the jetter. The wreck had been removed, but there still was a scar in the earth at the edge of the tall grass.

Hepzebah touched his arm. "It's done."

"No, it's just beginning."

Sil-Chan tipped his head toward an Admiral's shuttle which had landed at the end of the mowed strip and remained there without any

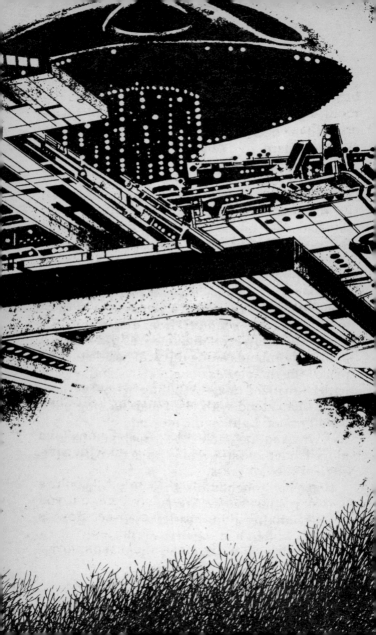

further sign of action. He glanced back into the room. There were at least twenty male Dornbakers in the room, all wearing sidearms. The woods around them, he knew were full of armed Dornbakers.

The PN had pulled off the broadcast without a change in script, but his manner had ignited worries in Sil-Chan's mind. Regal . . . remote . . . cold. The PN liked power, no doubt of that. Was he thinking about the power he might have as a planetary ruler? There had been a profound change in the PN's manner since his conference with his *Merlin.*

Merlin! Wizened little man with a leather bag of shiny pebbles and a covert look to him which said he had another bag full of shiny tricks.

"Who's in that shuttle?" Sil-Chan asked. "Why don't they come out?"

"What would you be doing?" she asked.

"Consulting with my government." Sil-Chan nodded.

"They've all heard the broadcast by now," she said. 'Sub-space must be burning up with communications."

"Tell me something," Sil-Chan said. "You're a primitive hunter-gatherer society here, but you know all about things like sub-space. How is that?"

"We're just naturally curious about your toys,"

she said. "The PN's the worst of the lot. He's got to see an example of everything. Some things we like and we use. Other things would change us too much and we reject them. That's the Pleb's main function—keep us culturally pure."

"Culturally . . ."

"That's why we have such severe limits on interchanging with the mainland. Damned little fraternizing."

"But it happens?"

She hugged him. "Sure it happens."

"Something's *happening* out there," he said.

She pulled away from him and they moved closer to the window. A hatch had opened on the Admiral's shuttle and a ramp tongued out to the ground. The PN and a small armed guard emerged from the woods beside the field and strode to a point opposite the ramp. When they stopped, men emerged from the shuttle—blue uniforms of the Galactic Navy and considerable glittering braid.

Sil-Chan recognized Perlig Ambroso, the head of the jackals, wearing the uniform of a captain in the Myrmid spacenavy. "Ahhh," Sil-Chan said.

"Something wrong?" Hepzebah asked.

"No. Something confirmed."

There was another smaller figure in the midst of the uniforms, someone in purple, but the press of military concealed this figure from Sil-Chan.

The military group stopped two paces from the PN and there was a short exchange of words.

Ominously, the shuttle's hatch closed, and weapons emerged from ports to threaten the area all around.

The PN did an about face and led the group toward David's house. Now, Sil-Chan could make out the purple-clad figure in the midst of the military: *Tchung!* The Director wore his official robes.

"That's Director Tchung," Sil-Chan whispered.

"I know," Hepzebah said. She turned away from Sil-Chan as the first of the group came to the door. David appared from somewhere and opened the door. The Admiral's group filed in first followed by Tchung and the PN's party. The Admiral was a florid faced man with button eyes. He stood almost as tall as the Pn.

As Tchung entered, Hepzebah bowed to him, said: "Good morrow to you, Cousin."

Sil-Chan gaped at her. *Cousin?*

Tchung returned her bow. "I greet the Elected Womb."

The PN turned at this exchange, addressed Tchung: "You were right and I was wrong, Cousin. You've a better eye than I thought. He's a man."

The Admiral was not ready for small talk. He

blustered: "Somebody had better explain this story about a debt against the Galactic Union! We are here investigating the costs of this boondoggle planet and any debts which . . ."

"One moment, please," the PN interrupted.

The Admiral frowned.

"A few minutes ago," the PN said, "I sent a private request to several members of the Galactic Union. I have demanded a General Assembly."

"Demanded?" The Admiral made no attempt to conceal his disdain. "You?"

"Demanded," the PN said. Regal, remote and cold.

"Only the leaders of sovereign planets can *demand* a General Assembly. This planet's a government bureau."

"*Was* a government bureau," the PN said.

As a sudden thought swept through his mind, Sil-Chan swept his gaze around the room, looking for the Merlin. Where was that wizened little plotter? Nowhere in sight.

The realized images of many faces began appearing at the rhomboid focus across the room. Sil-Chan abandoned his search for the Merlin and looked at the faces, recognizing many from the Directory of Planetary and System Rulers—Presidents, Dictators, Imperators, Regents . . . There was the Regent of Naos . . . and the Holy

Didactum of Jacun . . . the bloody little Messala of Hornaruth with her flat-lipped smile.

A larger focus at the center came alive with the round face of Hobart of Myrmid, Imperator of the Enclave, rulers of the Galactic Union. His features were flat, eyes bright and darting. The fact was oddly similar to that of Ambroso. *Related, perhaps?* Sil-Chan wondered.

The PN bowed to the Imperator. "We can begin."

There was a cold lump in Sil-Chan's stomach. *The PN's going to try for personal power!*

Hobart of Myrmid responded. His voice boomed out over the background crackling of subspace transmission. "My advistors have just informed me that this is an illegal calling of a General Assembly. The persons responsible will be arrested and confined in . . ."

"You'll hear me!" the PN bellowed. "I am the legal sovereign of this planet!" He took two strides toward the realized image.

The Admiral and guard moved to interfere, but froze as weapons appeared in the heads of the Dornbakers around the walls.

The PN said: "I have a legal claim against the Union for a sum that would drain your coffers."

"A mere technicality!" the Imperator shouted.

"You sovereign Assemblymen hear me," the PN said. "What you do to me could be done to

any of you. I propose a compromise. Confirm my sovereignty here and I will write 'Paid-in-full' on the debt you owe me.''

Anger boiled in Sil-Chan. He tugged Hepzebah several steps closer to the PN. "He's selling us out." Sil-Chan muttered.

Assemblymen were clamoring: "Explain! Explain!"

Hobart overrode the clamor: "This is no more than a technicality!"

"Hear him!" the Assemblymen shouted.

The PN strode even closer to the images as the rhomboid lenses tracked him. In the abrupt silence which ensued, he explained, finishing: "Is your Imperator a supreme dictator not answerable to the authority of the Assembly?"

"He rules by law!" one Assemblyman shouted. Others took it up: "By law! By law!"

The PN nodded. "Then I propose . . ."

Sil-Chan had taken enough. "You're being tricked!" he roared. He strode to the PN's side, dragging Hepzebah with him. Dornbaker weapons turned toward them.

"Who is this?" the Imperator demanded.

"I am an official of Galactic Archives!"

"This man has no authority here," the PN said.

Sil-Chan jerked credentials from his pocket, waved them at the lenses. The Imperator's gong intruded, bringing silence. Hobart of Myrmid

spoke in a stern voice:

"Let us hear this official of Galactic Archives. I, too, think we are being tricked."

"Hobart of Myrmid is one of those tricking you," Sil-Chan said.

It took twenty strokes of the gong to silence the bedlam of the Assemblymen. "Seize that man and hold him under arrest!" the Imperator roared.

But the room already was echoing with the voices of the Assemblymen. "No! No! Hear him! Hear him!"

Hobart of Myrmid hesitated.

Sil-Chan seized his opportunity: "I charge Hobart of Myrmid with planning to become absolute dictator of the Union."

Rapt silence greated this.

"I can prove that charge with Archives Records," Sil-Chan said. "Hobart of Myrmid plans to disband Galactic Archives and scatter the important pieces among his friends."

"You waste our substance!" the Imperator shouted. "Efficiency must come even to you!"

"And which planet gains monopoly of our weapons lore?" Sil-Chan demanded.

Assemblymen's faces bent closer.

"And who gets our physical sciences?" Sil-Chan asked. "The Planet Myrmid, perhaps?"

"He lies!" the Imperator screamed.

"The Assembly can send its own investigators," Sil-Chan said. "Then we will see who lies."

The Imperator gestured to the Admiral: "Silence that fool!"

Dornbaker weapons centered on the Admiral.

"Do you want control of these Archives to fall into the hands of a few ambitious men?" Sil-Chan asked.

An Assemblyman high on the right shouted: "If Archives is so dangerous, let's vaporize it!"

Sil-Chan said: "Which of you knows which files have been copied in recent months? Destroy the originals and the people with copies have it all their own way."

Silent faces stared at him.

"Renew our original charter but directly under the Assembly," Sil-Chan said. "You all know our impartiality. We are open to anyone. You are the real government and you know our Code: obedience to government."

"Truth! Truth! He is right!" the images roared. The yellow lights of affirmative votes filled the image areas. They cast a golden glow over David Dornbaker's living room.

"And give us a guardian patrol to protect us from a repetition of this incident!" Sil-Chan demanded.

Again, the room glowed yellow.

An Assemblyman in the high center addressed the Admiral: "Admiral! You will be held personally responsible for the Archives until the patrol arrives. Your life and the lives of all your officers are the price of failure!"

In the lower left bank of images, the Regent of Naos rang a chime. "Closed conference!" he called. The demand was repeated across the images.

The Imperator's image vanished. Others began to blank out. Soon all were blank.

The PN turned: "You took long enough before interrupting," he said. "I was beginning to wonder if we'd misjudged you."

"Mis . . ." Sil-Chan shook his head.

"It had to be natural and dramatic," Tchung said, moving up to Sil-Chan's left. "Very good."

"By the Stone," Hepzebah breathed. "A put-up!"

"I was afraid I might have to deal with an entire planet," the PN said. "I have enough trouble with my own family."

"And it would've destroyed one of the most precious things we've ever acquired," Tchung said.

Sil-Chan blinked at him.

"It would've destroyed a living, breathing primitive culture," Sil-Chan explained.

"These people?" Sil-Chan waved at the Dornbakers. "Primitive?"

"In their lifestyle," Tchung said. "They really are hunter-gatherers. Ohhh, they do use pretty good weapons, but not as sophisticated as they might."

"There's still the matter of all that dirt under us," the PN said.

Sil-Chan faced him. "That *dirt* is probably the largest untapped lodge of nickel-iron in this sector of the universe—enough to fuel Archives ships for thousands of years. I tried to tell you earlier. The magma was just cooled down and solidified."

"Pretty valuable, eh?" the PN asked. He nodded. "Well, we haven't settled that matter of the rest of our debt, either. Perhaps we . . ."

"Right now I think the Assembly would cede it to Archives directly," Sil-Chan said.

"Steal it from us?" the PN was outraged.

"We have provided increasingly costly services over all these centuries," Sil-Chan said.

"By contract!" the PN snapped.

"Perhaps," Sil-Chan said. "I think some good legal heads could tie the whole issue up for several centuries at least. There would be quite a bit of research to do, of course—right here. And we . . ."

The image of the Naos Regent appeared before the rhomboids and he said: "I beg to interrupt."

Sil-Chan and the others turned to face the

image. The Regent was an elderly, thin-faced man with suspiciously dark hair. Melanin tampering was indicated there . . . and a bit of masculine vanity, at least.

"I have the honor to be Jerem of Naos," he said, "the new Imperator of the Union. The Jeremiam Enclave renews the Archives charter under directorship of Patterson Tchung."

Tchung bowed. "We are honored."

"Formal investiture and official investigation of this unfortunate incident will take place soon," the new Imperator said.

Again, Tchung bowed.

The image vanished.

"We return to the uneasy truce between ignorance and knowledge," Tchung murmured. He smiled. "And I suspect we will gain a sudden influx of *students* doing special research."

The PN scowled. "What about the debt and all that . . . fuel under my island?"

Tchung shrugged: "Ohhhh, I think that can wait for a PN more favorably inclined toward Archives." He looked at Sil-Chan and Hepzebah. "It worked out rather well, don't you think? Much better than we expected."

"A put-up," Hepzebah muttered.

"Is he saying that our son could be PN?" Sil-Chan asked. "Our son would have that right?"

"By direct descent," she said. "We'll have to train him well."

AWARD-WINNING
Science Fiction!

The following titles are winners of the prestigious Nebula or Hugo Award for excellence in Science Fiction. A must for lovers of good science fiction everywhere!